# Contagion

## *Nature's Revenge*

## By David A. Umling

The author wishes to express his appreciation to the following people who contributed their guidance and assistance to the writing of this book:

*Technical Advisors:*

    Dale A. Carroll, *MD, MPH*

    Carroll Wayne Ours, *Retired Pharmaceutical Chemist, Abbott Labs, Chicago*

    Amanda Ours Barger, *B.S. Biology, Illinois State University, Normal, IL, 1997*

*General Editing Assistance:*

    Jeff Rhodes, Marina Oliver, Celeste Manning, and my loving wife, Barbara Umling

This book is dedicated to our remaining small family farms and the farmers who desperately struggle against all odds to keep them operating. The author also wishes to dedicate this book to the eternal spirit of Carroll Wayne Ours (June 1941 – August 2020) who contributed to this story and was a guiding star in my life.

# About this book and its author:

The day began like any other average day. Our lives were as we'd always known them to be, as we busied ourselves safe and secure in our confidence that it would all continue. Then, a tremendous explosion in the night set in motion a chain of events that would forever change our view of life and our place in nature. The very foundation of modern society was swept away from beneath our feet, revealing an apocalyptic world of hysteria, desperation, despair, and chaos that gradually destroyed all the glittering wealth and technological sophistication of the society we had built. Yet, from all the desolation, at least one family survives and prospers, having learned from the mistakes made by so many people who dared to imagine themselves as masters of the natural world that sustained them. Join David as he recounts the story of the great cataclysm and the subsequent changes it caused that restored nature's true dominion over humanity and reminded us of how we should live within it.

David lives with his wife of 29 years, Barbara, on Peeper Pond Farm in the northern Pendleton County community of Brushy Run, WV. Having lived the first 18 years of his life on a small family dairy farm, David has been an outspoken advocate for rural communities and their special needs throughout his 30-year professional planning career, from which he retired in 2017. He earned a Bachelor's Degree in Sociology and a Certificate in Applied Social Research from the University of Hartford, Connecticut in 1984 and a Master's Degree in City Planning from the University of California, Berkeley in 1986. In 2004, he received the Distinguished Leadership in Planning award from the Alabama Chapter of the American Planning Association. David is the author of three previous books, Lifestyle Lost (2012, Amazon Kindle), Reflections on My Lives: An Adoptee's Story (2014, Amazon Kindle), and Country Life at Peeper Pond Farm (2019, Amazon Kindle). David's posts on his farm website, www.peeperpondfarm.com, explain how to live more self-reliantly.

# Table of Contents

# Prelude

Humans are the most intelligent and adaptable living species on our planet. We are the only life form capable of dramatically transforming the natural world to serve our needs. No other species that has existed throughout the planet's history has so dominated and altered the Earth as we have. Yet, despite all that we have achieved and created, our greatest shortcoming and character flaw may be the inflated ego we internalized from our mighty intellect. That prideful sense of superiority allowed our species, in the name of compassion for our own sufferings or a perceived manifest destiny, to dominate and subdue nature to support human habitation and growth—even in the most remote areas of the Earth that are least capable of sustaining us, such as arid deserts and the frozen wastelands of the Arctic and Antarctic. While many people objected to the incidental extinctions that resulted from intense human competition for sensitive habitat areas, virtually no one extended those concerns to the most primitive and simple life forms (such as viruses and bacteria) that threaten our survival—even though *those* extinctions may have similar or even potentially greater consequences to alter the delicate balance of nature. Such is the basic nature of competition for survival among all living species, where each life form struggles and jostles to carve out its own niche. It's just that we humans possess certain intellectual and dexterous advantages that allow us to dominate the competition for Earth's limited resources, just as they often blind us to the potential repercussions.

Our advantages, in and of themselves, are not *necessarily* detrimental to the natural balance of life on Earth. Nature thrives on competition; it encourages the diversification of life. It is how we apply them and the decisions we make to use them that pose the greatest threat to the planet's natural resources. Unfortunately, our judgment in that regard is often clouded by the unbridled pride we feel for our intellectual and physical superiority.

That prideful arrogance was magnified and reinforced in the late twentieth and early twenty-first centuries by all the advanced technology and material wealth that the modern global economy created and the comforts and conveniences they bestowed upon burgeoning urban populations. All the while, our society marched forward driven by people who were determinedly confident in the power of their intellect and technology to solve any problem or answer any question they faced. We never stopped to consider how nature might fight back when the pressure became too great and resources were stretched too thin. We simply couldn't conceive that we might not be able to face that challenge. Why, we could just engineer another solution to it, whenever we felt it was necessary to do so.

However, nature had resources and weapons of its own that were so tiny and capable of such rapid reproduction that they could slip beneath our prideful arrogance and, in doing so, relevel the playing field. All that was necessary for nature to wage that war was the right triggering event that would set all the pieces in motion. For we humans and all our gleaming cities and technological advances, time had run out. Only those who learned the lessons nature had to teach us would survive.

Here beginneth the lesson...

# Part I.  *The Deadly Epidemic*

# 1. The Fateful Day

I knew this day would come.  I knew it *had* to come, just as it had for each of the prior generations.  Even so, it caught me by surprise when it did.  I had plenty of time to prepare for it, but it wasn't a pleasant thought to dwell on, so I procrastinated.  It's hard for me to know the best way to tell the horrific story to a child.

I didn't have to worry about it at all with my own children.  They were all born early enough in time that the lingering impacts from the cataclysm were still apparent on the landscape.  The great Appalachian forest that stretched behind our farm and across the summit of Cave Mountain remained broken and battered.  There weren't enough people and resources left behind to actively restore it.  The charred remains from periodic wildfires stood like blackened sentinels towering over the saplings that stretched skyward to replace them.  Starving wildlife occasionally staggered across our fields in a desperate search for food.  Many laid down to rest in our field and died during the long, dark winter nights.  The main highway below our farm was crumbling from neglect.  Isolated, lonely survivors from the big cities still wandered the roads (or what remained of them) seeking food, shelter, companionship, and some sense of hope.  My future wife was one of them.

We helped as many of them as we could, but we couldn't provide for them all.  Food demand from the survivors and the time we needed to replenish the fertility and productivity of our soil placed great constraints on our food stores during those early years.  Eventually, as time passed, the number of stragglers dwindled.  We don't know how many of them survived, but their decreasing numbers and frequency led us to presume that they were among the last to die.  These lingering effects made my eldest son (Michael) realize something terrible had happened before he was old enough to ask about it.  There was no avoiding the telling then.

Some sixteen years later, it was my grandchildren's turn to be told the story.  By then, many of the lingering effects had faded away into the recovering landscape.  The passers-by were long gone.  A new generation of trees on Cave Mountain had matured enough to hide the decaying remains of the older growth trees from casual view. Wildlife was beginning to recover rapidly with the natural restoration of the forest and the diminished human population to hunt them or compete with them. Our homestead farm operation had been gradually restored and expanded. Consequently, when an innocent slip of the tongue by Michael at the supper table caused his eldest son, eight-year-old Matthew, to ask pointed questions, the story had to be told. Unfortunately, the children were too young to comprehend it all, and each of them suffered from recurring nightmares about a prolonged disaster that was far beyond their experiences.

Our struggles to allay those nightmares, multiplied over five young grandchildren, made it apparent to us all that the telling of the saga had to be handled delicately, and even withheld until the children were old and experienced enough to understand life, death, and adversity. I guess I never invested enough thought into precisely *when* that time should be.

By the time Jeffrey, my first great grandson turned fifteen, another twenty-six years had lapsed from the prior generational telling, and we were all caught completely unprepared. A full sixty years had passed since the initial event that spawned the five-year catastrophe and forever changed the world I had known. Although I was only fifteen years old when it first occurred, the images of it remained fresh in my mind—burned indelibly into my memory like those charred remains of the dense, verdant forest that once towered majestically above our farm. How best to tell the story was the question I no longer had time to decide.

***** *****

The morning had begun innocently enough like any other average day. As I awoke, my eyes were met by the first rays of sunlight streaming through my bedroom window, as the sun began to break above the summit of Middle Mountain. Life on our farm was just beginning to stir. Michael was leading Essie, one of our eight Oberhasli dairy goats, into the milking barn to be milked. Her sister, Gertie, was standing at the gate of the goat pen watching him lead Essie away, as she bleated impatiently for her turn on the milking stand. The chickens, who had just been fed, were cackling, as they greedily pecked away at the freshly scattered feed. We also kept two horses, some hogs for meat in the fall, some sheep for wool and mutton, and some beehives for honey and candle wax. We lived as simply and self-reliantly as we could.

As I watched the scene from the front window of my cabin, Jeffrey emerged from the house and trudged across the yard to the goat barn in his homespun clothes and third-hand rubber boots, which wobbled loosely as he walked because they were still a couple sizes too large for his feet. It was his job to clean out the accumulated overnight goat poops from the barn, empty and refill the water buckets, and distribute hay and shelled corn for the goats to eat.

I stretched as I admired my view of the forested slopes of Cave Mountain. The new spring foliage glowed bright green as the leaves basked in the early morning sunlight. My focus on the beauty of the mountain was broken only by the melodious repertoire of a mockingbird that danced enthusiastically on one of the fenceposts lining the goat pen. Everything was as it should be.

I stirred the glowing embers in the potbelly wood stove that heated my simple two-room cabin and tossed in a stick of wood to revive the fire and ward off the early morning chill. Then I washed myself at the water basin and dressed for breakfast in the farmhouse. I would be spending the morning helping Kelly, Mike's wife, cultivate and plant the vegetable garden for the season.

I now lived alone in the small log cabin ever since my wife, Clara, had passed away three years ago. It afforded me some privacy from all the great grandchildren, even though I would spend most of the day in the farmhouse with Mike and his extended family. All of our lives were tied tightly to the 120-acre hardscrabble farm that sustained us. Although my other sons, Carl and Timothy and their respective wives and children, had moved away to work their own small, neighboring farms along the North Mill Creek valley, all of my great grandchildren received their daily schooling at our house. The members of our extended family were the only remaining people who now lived and farmed along the fifteen-mile-long valley. It was a full day's horse ride in any direction to reach our nearest unrelated neighbors.

To ensure our survival and satisfy as many of our basic needs as possible, our three adjoining family farms were designed to serve the most basic needs of each individual household as well as to provide specialized services that we all needed to survive, but couldn't commit the time, resources and labor to do individually. For instance, our farm produced enough milk to feed all three households, and we provided the homeschooling program that all of our children needed. Tim's farm, which was located on the flat, open lands across the creek from our farm, specialized in producing the hay, wheat and corn crops that we all needed to feed our livestock. Likewise, Carl's farm (which was located immediately upstream from our farm) operated a water-powered mill that could grind a portion of the wheat and corn that Tim's farm produced into flour to serve all our baking needs. The mill also provided a source of water power for Carl's forge, wood and metalworking shop that supplied us with all the lumber, horseshoes, hinges, latches, nails, and other essential materials we needed to repair and improve all of our farm buildings and equipment. In essence, our three adjoining farms served as a family-operated farm co-op to help efficiently divide and manage the most skilled and land-intensive needs that self-reliant living, without modern society, ultimately demands.

When I entered the front door of the farmhouse for breakfast, I was greeted by the familiar smell of eggs and cured bacon frying on the wood cookstove. Kelly, her shoulder-length auburn hair tied back into a simple pony tail, was setting the table, while Laura, Mike's and Kelly's daughter-in-law, was busy at the desk in the living room preparing the day's lessons for all of my great grandchildren.

After breakfast, Matthew and I harnessed and hitched our Morgan work horse, Hercules, to the single-blade plow, and I turned the soil in the garden. Having actively farmed throughout my life, I was physically capable of driving a horse and plow even in my advanced years. I then returned the plow, and we hitched Hercules to the spike harrow to loosen and smooth the soil for planting. Lastly, Mike spread a trash can full of woodstove and fireplace ashes across the garden, and I mixed it into the loose soil with a hoe to reduce the natural acidity level of the soil for the vegetables we intended to plant. By mid-morning, Kelly had joined me with the seeds we had carefully salvaged and dried from the prior year's crop. I hoed a series of planting row trenches and placed stakes at the ends of them as Kelly planted the vegetable seeds. We held back some of the seeds for later planting, so we could spread out our vegetable harvest throughout the growing season. With some additional help from Matthew, we watered in the freshly planted seeds.

By mid-day, the early season planting of the garden was finished, and we broke for a hearty dinner that Laura had prepared for us, after teaching the children their morning lessons. She had given them assignments to occupy their time while she prepared the meal for us. Such was the typical coordinated pattern of shared living that governed the course of our daily lives on the farm. Everyone had revolving roles to play, and everyone was cross-trained to perform the most basic chores so that an illness or injury would not disrupt the carefully choreographed daily pattern of life. It was the best and only way to survive self-reliantly in the new reality. It also reinforced strong family bonds across the generations, because we depended so strongly on each other to survive.

As the elder of our extended family, and the only member to have attended formal public schooling before the great cataclysm, it was my responsibility to review the children's "homework" with them during the afternoon. I would spend time with each child individually, beginning with the eldest and working my way down to the youngest. This order allowed the older children to be freed from their schooling responsibilities earlier in the day, so they could complete their afternoon farm chores before suppertime.

Jeffrey was the most inquisitive and enthusiastic outdoorsman of the four great grandchildren who still lived with me at our family farm. Of *all* my great grandchildren (now twelve in total), he had the greatest affection for farming and nature. He had raised two of our dairy goats on his own and cared for them as tenderly as he would if they had been his own children. He loved to hunt with his dad on Cave Mountain and would follow me on early evening walks to the small pond at the far edge of our hayfield to appreciate the annual raucous serenade of the spring peepers. When he was younger, he would challenge his brothers and sister on warm summer evenings to see who could catch the most fireflies in the hayfield, as they danced and sparkled like golden diamonds above the tall grass. Occasionally, I would see him from the front window of my cabin as he laid on the lawn admiring the stars in the night sky. He marveled at the sprawling, silky expanse of the Milky Way and, like the early Greek astronomers, discovered his own patterns in the starry sky.

Jeffrey's imagination and wonder about the puzzling workings of the natural world was unbounded. I had taught him much of what I had learned about basic astronomy, including the moon, stars, planets, and our galaxy, as they traced their nightly journeys across the sky above our valley. With the use of a candle (serving as the sun) and two round stones (representing the earth and the moon), I taught him how the moon's phases change from our perspective as we orbit about the sun. Like most people, he was stunned to learn how vast the universe was, and that most of the stars we see in the night sky are actually distant suns, similar to our own. It was no wonder to me why the night sky captivated him so. I had shared that fascination and wonder when I was a child. I guess it was only natural that he would come to me first with his questions about life and the fundamental mysteries of nature.

After working hard in the garden that day, I retired early to my cabin and sat quietly on the small front porch. I had briefly closed my eyes to absorb the comforting sounds of the night—specifically the crickets and a couple of whippoorwills deep in the woods calling plaintively for a mate—unfettered by the distracting evening activities and sights around me. Suddenly, I was startled by a gentle knock on a porch support post next to the steps. It was Jeffrey.

"Grandpa (as each of my great grandchildren called me), can I talk to you for a while?"

"Of course," I responded, pleased by his request. "What's on your mind this evening, son?"

"I was thinking about some things Mom taught us this morning, and I wanted to ask you some questions about it."

"Well, I'm not much of a teacher, but I'll see what I can do. "

Jeffrey hesitated a moment, as he collected his thoughts and sat down on the porch steps. Then he looked up at me and inquired, "How long has our family lived on this farm?"

"Oh, well now, let me think for a minute," I said as I rubbed my chin with my thumb and forefinger. "My father told me a long time ago that his great-great-great-grandfather bought this land and settled it exactly 40 years before West Virginia became a state, which would have been in……1823. I guess that would make you the ninth generation of our family to live on this farm." I smiled as I looked down at him, until I saw the puzzled look on his face. "Why do you ask?"

"I found a rock in the shale bank down by the pond last week that had an impression in it that looked like a leaf, but it wasn't one I'd ever seen before." At this point, Jeffrey reached into his pants pocket and produced the palm-sized fossilized rock he had found. He handed it to me as he continued, "I showed it to Mom, and she told me that it was a fossil from long ago—an impression made by an ancient leaf before the rock became hard like it is today. When I asked her why I can't find any leaves on our farm like it, she said it was because the ancient tree that made the leaf died out and doesn't exist here anymore. Over time, it was replaced by the different trees that we see today. I've seen lots of dead trees when Dad and I go hunting on Cave Mountain, but all of those trees are the same as the ones that are growing there today. Also, I've never seen a soft rock before, so I began to wonder how old this fossil might be. Since I knew our family has lived on this land for a long time, I thought maybe some of our ancestors would have been living here early enough to have seen those ancient trees. If they have changed that much, I thought one of them would have passed that information down, and you'd have heard about it."

I inspected his rock. It was a flat piece of black shale with a perfect impression of a small leaf on it. I could even see all of the tiny veins in the leaf. I didn't know what species it was either. I could almost see the depth of his inquisitiveness as he stared back at me. At that point, I decided he was probably old enough to comprehend the magnitude of past events. It was time to tell the story again.

"Jeffrey, the rock you found is very old. It's far older than anyone who ever lived here would remember. When I was young, people studied rocks like these and learned to tell how old they were. I don't know how to do it, and I don't know if there are any people alive today who would remember how. That knowledge disappeared when I was about your age. Things have changed dramatically in my lifetime, and I think it's time I told you about it. The way you're thinking, you'd probably soon realize that we haven't been telling you everything you should know about the past. Let's go in the cabin, and I'll tell you the story."

I picked up my chair and carried it into the cabin. Jeffrey followed me, closed the door, and took a seat at the small table in the center of the room. I took a couple of beeswax candles off the shelf, struck a match, lit them, and set them down between us on the table. As our shadows danced along the cabin walls in the flickering candlelight, I began the tale of the great cataclysm that forever changed our world.

# 2. The Meteor

"I know that the story I have to tell you will be shocking to hear. When I told your dad about it nearly thirty years ago, he had a lot of nightmares. Of course, he was only eight years old then, but it's hard to accept and understand it all when everything that happened is so far beyond anything you've ever known or experienced. It will take some time to tell you about it all because it happened over a number of years. I just want you to ask me any questions you need to ask to understand it. Just don't live in fear of it all. It happened a long time ago, and there's little chance that you'll ever have to live through anything like it again. I just want you to learn the lessons that the story has to teach us about the natural world and how we should live in it. If only the people who lived before it had all understood that, it might not have been as catastrophic as it was, but if you learn from it, I think you'll enjoy a richer and more satisfying life. Do you think you can do that?"

Jeffrey sensed the seriousness and concern in my voice, and I watched him think carefully about the meaning of my words. "I'll try, Grandpa. I won't be afraid if *you* tell it to me. I'd like to know about it."

I gave him a reassuring smile and settled back in my chair. Then, I began...

"All of this happened about sixty years ago—when I was your age. It was a very different time. The world seemed much bigger than it does today. First of all, there were many more people living in it than you've ever seen in your life. There were cities—many of them. Although none of the cities in our area were big, there was a small town at the lower end of our valley that was called Petersburg. About 2,500 people lived there. In the opposite direction from us was Franklin. Roughly 700 people lived there. Stretched along the valley road that ran between them were scattered farms and homes. Your aunts and uncles moved into some of them when they began to have children of their own. The rest just collapsed over time and are hidden in the woods that have grown up around them. There weren't enough people left behind to live in and maintain them all. If you look closely, though, you'll find foundations, cellar holes, and maybe a few partial walls hidden in the trees and brush. Over time, we salvaged materials from some of them to repair and build up our own farms."

At this point, Jeffrey's eyes opened wide and he exclaimed, "I think I saw one of them once when my dad took me hunting on Cave Mountain last fall! It was a big rectangular hole in the ground lined with rocks. I found some rotten wood and other scraps in it. When I showed it to him, Dad said it was just an old house that the owners abandoned when they moved away. I asked him why someone else didn't move into it, and he told me that it was probably so old and run down that no one wanted it. He said he'd found more of them scattered about the forest, but he never told me why all the people left." His interest was now piqued, and he asked eagerly, "How many cities were there? How many people lived in them?"

"I don't know for sure how many cities there were around the world, but there were many of them. It's hard for you to imagine this, but remember when I told you how many stars there may be in the sky?"

"Yes," Jeffrey immediately replied, "I remember. You said there were billions of them in our galaxy and billions of galaxies beyond them in the universe. Then you told me how big a number that was."

"Right. Well, there were billions of people living all around the world. Millions of them lived in and around the biggest cities, some of which could be reached within a day before all the roads crumbled away. Here. Wait just a second, and I'll show you something."

I got up from my chair and went into the bedroom. I opened the large cedar chest that stood at the end of my bed and rifled through the quilts and old keepsakes stored in it. On the bottom left side of the chest, I removed an old shoebox and brought it back to the table. I removed the lid and carefully removed some old, worn postcards with pictures of the New York City skyline and various government buildings and monuments in Washington, DC. I explained what they were as I handed them to him for closer inspection.

"This is a picture of the biggest city in our nation. It was called New York City, and it was home to more than twenty million people."

Jeffrey gazed wide-eyed at all the skyscrapers that lined the Hudson River. "I've never seen buildings like these, Grandpa. How tall were they?"

"The tallest of them had 100 or more floors and stood well over 1,000 feet high. When you walked along the roads in that city, they towered above you, just like our mountains do when you walk along the river in Smoke Hole Canyon. People lived and worked in all those buildings. Here's another picture of one of the city streets all lit up at night. Just look at all the people you see walking about. That's how crowded that city used to feel."

Jeffrey was clearly amazed. He'd never seen so many people in one place at one time in his entire life. As he looked up at me, speechless, I handed him some postcards of Washington, DC.

"Jeffrey, these are pictures from another city called Washington. It was the capital city of our entire nation—of which our West Virginia was only a small part. Washington never had the tall buildings you see in New York City, but it had lots of important government buildings, museums, and monuments that represented the history of our nation. Do you remember your great grandma?" Jeffrey nodded in reply. "Well, these old pictures I'm showing you belonged to her. She and her family lived near Washington before the great disaster. She left with her parents during the aftermath, and they came by our farm looking for shelter and food. They left her with us until they found a new place for her because they knew we had food and would take care of her while they were gone. We never knew what happened to them, because they never returned. Maybe they starved like so many of the other survivors. Maybe they were robbed and killed by desperate scavengers. Maybe they just left her with us because they knew they couldn't give her the life we could. We just don't know. Anyway, I eventually married her, and she stayed with us for the rest of her life. I just don't have answers for everything that happened in those times."

I watched quietly as Jeffrey thumbed through the postcards engrossed with the images they contained of places and things that were beyond his youthful imagination. I sat silently for a few moments to let him absorb the images, then I continued.

"If you look at the pictures carefully, you'll see motorized vehicles in the roads. They were called automobiles. People drove them to get around. They could travel much faster than our horses at full gallop. If you ever go to those places, you may see some of them rotting and rusting along the roads. They became useless when the world economy collapsed, and the supply of liquid fuel they needed was cut off. That only made life in the cities even harder on the people who lived in them.

"City people didn't live or work on farms. They worked in all those big buildings you see in the pictures. There was no room in those cities for people to farm or keep livestock. Country farmers like us grew and raised all the food they needed and sent it to the cities so they could spend their time building machines, making clothes, selling goods, or serving all the other basic needs of city people. These cities existed for many generations, and people became dependent on the businesses in them to give them jobs to earn money, which they then used to pay for all the food, goods, and services they needed to live, but couldn't produce for themselves."

Having said that, I removed a few old, tattered dollar bills from the box and handed them to him. Jeffrey accepted them silently and began to study them as I continued. "That's what the money they used looked like. It became so important to have it that people eventually became greedy for it. Some people craved so much of it that their whole self-esteem was measured by how much money they possessed. Those who had more money than they needed to support themselves often looked down upon those who had very little. When the cities began to collapse, all the money became worthless, which made people more desperate to survive.

"Over many generations, most city people became dependent on all the lifestyle conveniences and labor-saving devices they could buy with their money and forgot (or never knew) where their food came from or how it was produced. That's why so many of them couldn't survive when the world economy and the cities collapsed. They just didn't know how to survive on their own as we do. You'll understand all this better after I tell you how it all started and evolved over time."

Jeffrey looked up at me, and I could see the bewilderment in his eyes. This was a lot of new information for him to absorb. The idea of cities, skyscrapers, money, automobiles, and people who never lived on a farm was way beyond his experience and strained his comprehension. All he could say in response was, "I never knew about all these things."

"I know, Jeffrey," I said reassuringly. "It's a lot for you to digest. That's why I said life before the great catastrophe was very different than the one that we live today. But that's the way it was, and it's important for you to have some idea of how much it changed. Only then can you appreciate how devastating the events that caused the collapse were and how they built upon themselves. Don't worry about understanding everything I've said about the way people lived back then. Just understand all these changes were caused by one very rare event. Do you want me to continue, or do you want to think some more before I begin the tale?"

Once I asked the question, I saw Jeffrey's eyes refocus on me. "Please, Grandpa, tell me some more. I don't think I could get to sleep wondering what else you have to tell. I want to know."

I smiled at him as he handed me the postcards and currency. I carefully put them back in the shoebox and replaced the lid. Then I drew a deep breath and began the story about the day the meteor fell.

***** *****

"I remember that summer night clearly in my mind, even though it occurred so long ago. We had just finished a long day of loading hay in the barn, and we were very tired. We hadn't been asleep very long when a tremendous explosion—louder than any thunder we'd ever heard before—

woke us up.  It was so loud, it shook the whole house, and it continued to shake hard as the rumble echoed throughout the valley.  We all got out of bed and stumbled into the living room.  All the younger children were crying.  My dad told Mom to take the kids into the central bathroom, which was the safest interior room in the house.  He instinctively grabbed his rifle and some ammunition and told me to follow him onto the front porch.

"By the time we got out on the porch, the echo of the explosion had passed and the shaking subsided.  It was deathly quiet.  Even the livestock was stunned by fear and unwilling to make a sound.  I looked up at the sky over Middle Mountain.  It was clear, and all the stars were shining brightly.  We soon became aware that there was a dull glow behind the house, over Cave Mountain.  When we looked around the corner of the porch, it appeared to cast a greenish yellow glow along the ridgeline that wavered softly in brightness, like a window sheer rippling gently in a light summer breeze.  I asked Dad what he thought it was, but he didn't have an answer.  We just stood there together at the north end of the porch watching the glow flutter for what seemed like many minutes.  Then, I saw Dad cock his head slightly as he asked, 'Do you hear that?'

"I listened closely and I thought I could hear a dull roar building over the mountain, like a strong wind approaching us from the northwest.  Oddly enough, there didn't seem to be a breath of air moving where we were standing.  It just got louder and louder, as though it was racing toward us.  Then, I noticed how the glow along the ridgeline started to disappear behind a layer of blackness that was rising slowly up into the sky.  As the roar got louder and louder, the blanket of black rose higher and higher until the glow was so obscured that we couldn't distinguish it from the starry night sky.  Then, the stars began to disappear and the approaching roar became deafening.  I wanted to run and hide, but there seemed to be no place to go, and I was frozen by the fear welling up inside me.

"I heard Dad say with great concern in his voice, 'This doesn't sound good at all.'  Then he grabbed my arm and pulled me back from the end of the porch. We crouched down at the base of the house wall and waited momentarily for the ferocious shock wave to approach. It didn't take long.

"We could hear it crest the summit of Cave Mountain. As it descended the slopes of the mountain, we heard the sound of mighty trees snapping and popping as though they were mere twigs. When it finally hit our house, it felt like the mountain itself was colliding with us. The house jolted hard again and began to creak and groan under the stress. The air wrapped around the ends of the porch and hit us like a blast furnace. It felt so hot that I could hardly breathe or open my eyes. It roared with such force as it swept through our farm that I could hear it ripping the roofing off and blowing heavy debris into the back side of the house and across the yard. Suddenly, I realized I could hear the barn being ripped apart. On and on that wind howled for what seemed like an hour, but I knew it must have been only a few minutes. As it began to subside, I caught my breath and opened my eyes. It wouldn't completely subside for more than fifteen minutes.

"We knew the house had been damaged, but it hadn't blown away. We stood up slowly and tried to survey the damage from the porch. It was then that I realized all of the stars were gone. The curtain of blackness that I saw rising over the mountain had also swept across us with the furious wind. As if compelled by a reflex, I sniffed the air. It smelled to me like a coal furnace, and I began to cough as the foul odor filled my lungs. Dad also began coughing, as we struggled to choke down the acrid air. It was so strong we had to retreat into the house. At least the charcoal smell of the air was not as strong inside. We could hear the children screaming and crying with fear in the bathroom. Dad called out to Mom and promptly, they all emerged one by one. We gathered in the center of the living room and hugged each other as tightly as we could, while we waited for the outside air to settle down.

"Finally, we began to look up at each other as Dad asked if we were all right. We couldn't see each other clearly because of the intense darkness in the room. Mom carefully felt her way to the fireplace mantel, took down an oil lantern, and lit it. The younger kids were still whimpering as they choked back their remaining tears, when Mom stared at Dad's and my faces and said,

'You look like you're covered with soot.' As we separated, it became obvious that Dad and I were covered in the blackest coat of greasy soot that you could imagine. It looked as though we had just returned home from working in a coal mine. Mom also noted that our hair and eyebrows appeared to have been singed. It was true. I even had some heat blisters on the back of my hands, which I had used to cover my face while I struggled against the intense blast of hot air.

"None of us could get any more sleep that night. We shivered with fear every time we heard the house creak or crack as it resettled from all the stress it had withstood. We wanted to run, but we were more afraid of what we might see outside. What's more, we had nowhere else to run. If the house was going to fall on us, it might be the best way to die. Fortunately, it didn't. We just sat on the living room floor and waited for time to decide our fate. Mom told us to pray for everyone's safety and the return of daylight.

"Eventually, we noticed that the room was getting brighter. The sky had not cleared, but the sun had already risen. The sky assumed a ruddy reddish-brown color as the low cloud cover was illuminated from behind by the sun. The outside air had cooled, but it still felt warm for that time of the day. At least the caustic odor had either dissipated or lifted to higher altitudes, and only a light, smoky smell remained. That smell would linger for days as the smoldering remains of charred trees in the forest slowly burned out.

"When we finally corralled the courage to leave the house and go into the front yard, the scene was distressing. The yards were littered with debris, from burned, lifeless tree branches to bricks blown from the chimney and shingles ripped from the roof. There, scattered around the yard, were scores of shattered and splintered boards—perhaps ripped from one of our buildings or swept off the mountain from other homes in the path of the shock wave. Several broken boards had been impaled into the windward side of the house. Fortunately for us, no windows were broken. Despite all the damage, the house appeared to be largely intact, but our livestock barn was gone and the lifeless bodies of our horses and bulls were laying at the edge of the woods below us. We never did find the chicken coop or any of our chickens that had roosted in it for the night. It would take many months of hard work to repair all the damage.

"All the other farms in our valley sustained similar damage or worse. Hundreds of people in our area died from the initial shock wave. Some of the survivors lost their hearing from the explosion, but we were more fortunate. All of us survived the great blast with little more than minor cuts, bruises, and burns. It would be days before we learned what had caused it. According to all the preliminary reports we heard, a stony asteroid roughly 250 feet wide had exploded over the Allegheny Front, about sixty or so miles northwest of our farm. It had leveled or burned most of the forest on the high plateau and instantly killed more than ten thousand people, even though it never hit the ground. It exploded about ten miles up in the sky. It was said that if the meteor had exploded over Washington (only 150 miles farther along its flight path) over two million people would have died. I guess that was supposed to make us feel lucky.

"There was one interesting and important fact about the meteor that was not revealed to the public for many weeks after it exploded. The asteroid's flight path and speed had been calculated as it approached the Earth. Since it was traveling far faster than the maximum speed it could travel to be held in orbit around the sun, it was determined that the asteroid was from outside our solar system. It had travelled for many millions and perhaps billions of years from some other star system. This seemingly incidental piece of information would have grave consequences for future events as the catastrophe expanded and continued to unfold."

The expression on Jeffrey's face reflected his awe and captivation as I concluded the story of the night the interstellar meteor exploded over West Virginia. He was simply spellbound. I watched as the story soaked in. He looked into my eyes and simply said, "That's the most incredible story I've ever heard. I don't know what to say about it."

I looked back at him with a reassuring smile and said, "I do, Jeffrey. It's time for you to go to bed. Understand, though—that's just the beginning. I'll tell you the rest of the story tomorrow after you've had some sleep. Hopefully, you won't spend the whole night thinking about it. Now you go on into the house and tell your papa (which was the name Jeffrey used for my son, Mike—his grandfather) to come out here and talk to me. I need to let him know that I'm telling you the story."

With that, I ushered him out the door and sat back down at the table until I heard my son knock gently on the cabin door.

# 3. Studying the Impact

When I entered the farmhouse for breakfast the next morning, Mike had already informed Kelly, Laura, and Matthew that I had started telling Jeffrey about the great cataclysm. At first, Laura and Matthew were concerned about it, until they heard what had brought it about. They all eventually agreed that it was probably time for him to know. As we enjoyed our breakfast of sausage gravy and fresh wheat biscuits, we discussed how the day's chores could be rearranged and reassigned so that Jeffrey and I could go fishing in Smoke Hole Canyon while I finished telling the tale. Jeffrey was *always* eager to go fishing.

After breakfast, Matthew harnessed Prince, our Morgan gelding, to our one-horse shay, while Jeffrey and I loaded our fishing poles, bait, net, a five-gallon bucket, and tackle into it. Laura ordered us to return with a good string of fish for supper, and reminded us sternly that we would be responsible for cleaning them. Kelly packed a lunch basket for us containing deviled eggs, cheddar cheese slices, honey cornbread, some deer jerky, and a couple of apples with a half-gallon mason jar of spring water to wash it all down. Jeffrey knew it would be a memorable trip, and that knowledge made him proud. So much so, that as we started off, I saw Jeffrey covertly stick his tongue out at his younger brother, John, who had just started helping Mike and Matthew shear the sheep. That was to have been Jeffrey's morning job.

It was a beautiful, sunny spring day to go fishing. Wild plum trees were in full bloom, as were dense patches of phlox lining the shoreline of the creek and the old Petersburg Pike. Even Prince seemed to be energized by the bright, colorful scene as he maintained a sprightly trot. For me, the serenity of the day was a stark contrast to my memories of the dark days after the meteor exploded. It was a 45-minute ride to our favored fishing spot at the base of Eagle Rock, so I decided to resume my telling of the story.

"Did you sleep well last night?" I asked to gently break the peaceful silence.

"I didn't have any nightmares, if that's what you mean. It took me a while to get to sleep because I kept thinking about everything you told me. I was anxious to know what happened next. But once I finally got to sleep, I didn't wake up until sunrise."

"That's good to hear. I know it captivates your mind and you're eager to hear the rest of the story, but it's going to take some time to explain it all. I hope you can be patient with me. I don't want the story to keep us from enjoying our fishing trip."

"Don't worry, Grandpa. It will all be part of the fun. I've seen our animals die, and I've helped you and Papa slaughter our hogs and chickens. I'm not afraid to know the rest of the story, no matter how gruesome it may be."

"Good. Then I'll continue. When the meteor exploded, it scorched a large area on the Allegheny Plateau in both Maryland and West Virginia. The trees, undergrowth, and soil compost smoldered for many days. All the lingering heat and foul smoke made it difficult and dangerous to investigate the impact area. Even the skies above our farm were hazy with smoke carried by the prevailing winds.

"The first inspection of the impact zone was done from the air. From what they could see through the smoky haze, the explosion destroyed a large oval section of forest on the mountain that was at least thirty miles long and twenty miles wide. Several small communities on the plateau in West Virginia and far western Maryland were completely destroyed, which accounted for most of the initial deaths. Near the center of the debris field, the area referred to as 'ground zero,' they found a circular area several miles across where all the trees had been burned, but the broken trunks were still standing upright. They determined that was the spot directly beneath the explosion because all the rest of the trees outside ground zero were laid out flat on the ground in a pattern that pointed away from the central blast, as the shock wave radiated outward in all directions.

"The first ground investigation targeted the ground zero zone. The scientists were searching for fragments of the meteor to analyze, and they expected to find the highest concentration of them in the area directly below the explosion. However, they weren't able to find any recognizable pieces of the actual meteor. They decided that the original meteor must have been very stony, which made any fragments that survived the explosion very small and hard to locate and even more difficult to distinguish from many of the native rocks that had been scorched and even melted by the intense heat of the explosion. Also, the ground in that part of the Allegheny Plateau is very wet and swampy, so most of the remnants would have been driven deep into the mucky soil by the force of the explosion.

"It would take a lot of time and intensive survey work for them to collect the rock samples they were seeking. In fact, because the weather on the plateau was so harsh and unpredictable, the search process took much longer than they anticipated. It took more than a month before they were able to draw any preliminary conclusions about the actual composition of the meteor. They eventually concluded that the meteor probably formed from the debris of a collision of two or more other asteroids or planets. The mineral composition of the fragments they eventually found differed among themselves and from the rocks that are commonly found on the plateau. They were loosely bound together by ice and dust, which is why it exploded from the frictional heat it generated as it streaked through our atmosphere only seconds before it would have struck the ground.

"Unfortunately, all the early analysis of the meteor fragments was focused on the geology of the fragments, so they did not give much attention to the biological aspects of the rocks. Some of the scientists assumed that the intense heat of entry into our atmosphere and the resulting explosion prior to impact would have vaporized or killed any biological elements that might have been contained in the small, residual fragments they found. Still other scientists dismissed a biological analysis because it took so long to find the fragments that they would have been contaminated by earthly organisms in the soil where they landed. Those may have been reasonable assumptions to make at the time, but they eventually proved to be wrong. The rocks that made up the asteroid did indeed contain biological matter from at least one of the colliding bodies from which it had formed—and that the organic matter in the meteor came from *outside* our solar system!"

I saw Jeffrey's eyes widen when I made that statement. Farmers certainly can't claim to be experts in biology, but they do learn a lot about it from working closely with animals and nature. Jeffrey had learned about germs and bacteria from all our illnesses and those of our livestock. He knew why we had to cure our meat in order to preserve it. He also understood how plants, animals, and humans reproduce. You can't be a successful farmer unless you learn these basic aspects of life. When he heard me say that the asteroid had delivered organic matter to Earth from beyond our solar system, he immediately recognized that could be an important problem. A frown formed on his face as he said, "If these people were as smart as they appear to be, why didn't they consider that possibility more carefully?"

"That's a good question. I wish I had an equally good answer to give you. After all, the people who lived in that time had a lot of knowledge about outer space and the planets in our solar system. They had built many sophisticated automated rocket-probes that were sent into space and returned pictures and even data from *all* the known planets in our solar system, including several we can't see in the sky at night because they are so far away. What you also don't know is that many people (men and women) had traveled into space. Twelve of them actually walked on the moon and returned soil and rock samples with them to Earth. In the final decades before the meteor fell, our society was preparing to send the first humans to Mars.

"Back in those days, most people had a basic understanding of the solar system and our place in it. They also learned that most of the stars we see in the night sky have solar systems of their own. Thousands of planets orbiting around distant stars had been identified and catalogued. Even the thought of life on other planets outside our solar system was broadly accepted. Many people believed that any other life forms as intelligent or more intelligent than us would not be dangerous to us, because they would understand how fragile and special all life is. However, another segment of the population believed that outside life forms could be envious of our planet and its resources and, therefore, might constitute a threat to us.  Some people even believed that some of these alien life forms had already visited our planet, despite common knowledge that the distance between the stars was too great to be travelled in hundreds of human lifespans.  Given all the complexities and practical limitations of space travel to other stars, it is not likely that we, or even any other more advanced life forms, if they do exist, could ever accomplish it.

"Even though a significant segment of the population believed life existed on other planets, that some of those beings were more advanced than us, and that they could eventually find a way to travel the immense distance to reach our world, they were far less concerned about any potential threat from simple, microscopic alien life forms.  I guess that's because they learned that none of the early astronauts who went into space or traveled to the moon ever got infected by microbes in space and none were ever discovered in the moon rocks that they brought back with them.  They eventually concluded that intense radiation levels in space would kill most unprotected life forms.  I guess that's ultimately why most people presumed that alien life forms traveling to Earth would have to be advanced enough to build spaceships that would protect and sustain them on the desperately long voyage.

"However, some biologists were gradually discovering some primitive, microscopic life forms on Earth that *could* survive incredibly hot and cold temperatures and exposure to intense radiation—even with no protection. Biologists also knew of many life forms on Earth that don't require any air to survive.  Those insights made it much more likely (under the right circumstances) that the most simple and primitive organisms could better survive long interstellar flights through space than more complex and advanced life forms like us, who need to carry with them all the food, air, and stable climate they would need to survive.  However, that perspective was so new that most people never thoroughly understood it.  They simply continued to cling to the accepted idea that only highly intelligent and technologically advanced life forms like ourselves could survive long-distance space travel.

They just never seriously entertained the possibility that the opposite might actually be far more plausible.

"Since the first scientists who investigated the meteor impact site were geologists, and the impact conditions weren't very conducive to the survival of alien microbes, the possibility of finding alien organisms in the meteor debris just wasn't seriously reconsidered until later evidence began to mount that their initial presumptions were wrong. In essence, it may have been an error caused by intellectual vanity. As I look back on it, I believe they simply *thought* they knew more than they had *proved* they knew."

Jeffrey nodded to me. "My dad once told me that ignorance was far easier to come by than intelligence."

"Yes," I chuckled. "That's a good way to understand it."

"So, what happened to make them realize that the meteor contained microbes from another solar system?" Jeffrey asked.

"I really don't know how long it took them to seriously consider it, but the first evidence came from some of my father's friends who helped lead the initial scientists to the ground zero site. As they traveled around the stark, ravaged landscape during the first few weeks following the impact, they eventually began to find small pools of stagnant water that were covered by an orange scum unfamiliar to them. Some of them claimed that they noticed thin hair-like strands—like very thin, primitive veins or roots—radiating throughout the scum layers. At first, they thought it was just an exotic form of algae that grew in response to the impact conditions. However, most of the algae the locals typically found in the area was green or turquoise in color, like the algae you see forming in our farm pond during the summer. None of them could remember finding an orange scum. They also didn't see any of it outside of the impact zone. They didn't fear it at the time; they just stepped around it and went about their business. Eventually, however, the scientists began to take an interest in the odd colored algae. By that time, it was already too late."

At this point in the story, we had reached the road that led into Smoke Hole. I tugged gently on the right rein and issued the command for Prince to gee. He obediently veered right onto Smoke Hole Road, and we started down along the South Branch River into the canyon. The road quickly narrowed and I told Jeffrey that I needed to concentrate on the road until we got to Eagle Rocks. The narrow passage between the hillside cliffs on the left side of the road and the sheer drop to the river below on the right made it dangerous to divert my attention from the road even for brief periods of time. All along the way, we heard the mighty thunder of the river rushing over the jumble of giant rocks and boulders hundreds of feet below us, as torrents of water squeezed through the narrow gorge.

We passed the time with idle conversation about the trout we planned to catch, until the massive rocky pinnacle of Eagle Rocks eventually appeared before us. I pulled Prince onto a wide shoulder along the road and commanded him to stop. We retrieved all of our fishing gear from the shay and picked a good, sheltered, shady spot immediately downstream from a rocky cataract that had always proven to be a fine spot to catch brown and rainbow trout. We picked out a couple of good riverside boulders to sit on, filled the bucket we brought with fresh river water, and baited our lines.

# 4. The Contagion

We had just started fishing, when I noticed Jeffrey was tugging a little too hard on his line. "Be gentle with it, Jeffrey," I said softly. "Don't get too eager. Remember trout are very finicky eaters. They don't snap at the first thing they see like many other fish. You need to tease them to take the bait. If you pull the line too fast, you'll scare them off. Just pull the line along slowly, a little bit at a time. Let them notice the bait and take an interest in it. Don't snap your line as soon as you feel them nibble. Wait until they've decided it's good to eat, and then snap the line to hook them."

"I will, Grandpa. It's been a long time since I fished for trout. Dad usually takes me to South Mill Creek Lake to fish for bass. Is this your favorite fishing spot?"

"I used to fish here a lot when I was your age. Now that I think about it, it's been quite a few years since I last came here. It's about six miles from our farm, so I haven't had the time to come this far just to fish. However, it's always been my favorite spot to catch trout. They like to live just downstream from a cataract like the one back there. The water picks up a lot of oxygen from the air as it cascades over the rocks. The canyon walls are very narrow here, which gives it a lot of shade. That means the water stays cool—the way they like it. If the trout are good and hungry, as they should be early in the morning, we should do well."

As if responding to my command, I felt the first tenuous nibble on my line. Jeffrey became quiet and still when he saw me tease the fish with gentle tugs on my line. I felt a few more quick nibbles, then snapped my line hard, successfully snagging the fish on my treble hook. As I began reeling him in, the monster leapt above the surface, thrashing desperately, as he sought to free himself. I was concerned that he might break the line. We had to be very careful with our fishing supplies, because we couldn't make them on our own. All we had to use were the supplies we could salvage from the time of the meteor impact. Fortunately, the line and hook held, as I reeled him in. He was a magnificent rainbow trout. Jeffrey propped his pole against some rocks and scrambled to grab the net. He lowered it before me just as I lifted our trophy from the river. It writhed in the net for a few moments before peacefully succumbing to its fate.

I told Jeffrey that the fish was much too large to keep in the bucket. We intended to use the bucket as a holding tank for smaller fish, so we could decide which of them to keep and which to release, depending on the number and size of the fish we eventually caught. Any small fish we didn't need would be returned to the river so they could grow big for a future fishing trip, like the trophy I had just caught. He must have weighed at least eighteen pounds.

I lifted the big trout out of the net and told Jeffrey to give me the string line in the tackle box. I mounted him on one of the bottom hooks, looped the string tightly around a strong shoreline branch to hold it, and dangled the dead fish in a placid, shallow eddy along the shore. That would keep him fresh for the rest of our stay. "Well, Jeffrey, we've landed our first trophy fish. What do you think about that?"

"Wow! You sure made that look easy, Grandpa. I can't wait to catch one of my own."

"Don't worry about rushing things, Jeffrey. We've got the whole day ahead of us. We just have to keep fishing. You never know what you're going to catch, but this is a really good start."

Having dealt with the fish I caught, I baited my line again and sat down next to Jeffrey, who had already resumed working his line. Once I had cast my line into the shallow pool immediately downstream of some riffles, Jeffrey looked at me and sheepishly implored, "Aren't you going to continue with the story, Grandpa?"

"Oh? Wouldn't you rather just spend some time with me enjoying the sounds of the river and concentrating on your fishing?" He instantly knew I was teasing him.

"Grandpa! You know I want to hear what happened with the orange algae from the meteor. Can't you just tell me while we're fishing?"

"Well, it's a little complicated. For the first week of the search for meteor fragments, they struggled to find anything. The scattered pools of orange scum didn't even begin to form until about two weeks into the search. Even when they did begin to appear, they weren't considered a high research priority. There were a number of small surface coal mines in that area of the plateau, so some of the scientists may have thought the orange pools resulted from residual acids stirred up by the explosion that were once used by the mining companies to remove impurities from the coal. After all, those acids were known to cast a yellow-orange tint in water that drains out of old mine seams. That might explain why the scientists just worked around them. Some additional clues had to emerge before they decided to refocus their research.

"Do you remember when I told you that my dad and I were coated in a black soot on the night of the explosion?"

"Yes. Wasn't that just ash from the explosion?"

"It was. At least, that's what we concluded. We just changed our clothes and washed it off the next morning shortly after daybreak. Then we went about our work to assess the damage and clean up the debris left behind by the shock wave. We were so busy with our initial recovery and repair work that we didn't give it another thought. That is, until about a week later when Dad and I began to feel ill. It started as a nagging cough and a scratchy throat. Then we noticed that the cuts and burns we had on our hands and faces weren't healing well and were showing signs of infection.

"We just assumed it wasn't serious because the clean-up work was such a dirty business. That's all we thought about it at the time. Fortunately, Mom was an expert on medicinal plants and natural medicine. She collected medicinal plants from our fields and forests and prepared all sorts of tinctures, salves, and herbal teas to treat whatever ailed us. She applied some elder leaf salve to our cuts and burns and covered them with cloth bandages. Then she gave each of us each a dose of elderberry tincture and mullein tea for our cough and sore throat and sent us to bed early for some extra rest. We were just too poor to run to a doctor every time we had a cold or a simple infection. However, the next morning, we awoke with strong headaches and stiff muscles, especially in the backs of our necks. We were also showing signs of fever.

"At this point, Mom realized this could be a severe flu that she couldn't control with her simple herbs and wildflower remedies. She contacted Uncle Bob, my dad's brother, because he was a doctor who worked at the Petersburg Memorial Hospital. Mom knew he wouldn't charge us full price for his services. She called it our 'family discount.' More often than not, he treated us for free at home.

"During the first several months after the impact, the Petersburg hospital was the only medical facility in the immediate area of the impact zone that was still operating. The other nearby hospitals in Oakland, Maryland and Keyser, West Virginia were closer to ground zero and were heavily damaged by the blast. All immediate medical needs throughout the region were being directed to Petersburg for preliminary diagnosis and then referred to larger, more distant hospitals as required for specialized treatment.

"Uncle Bob knew we had all survived the initial impact, but when he heard that Dad and I had taken ill, he rushed to our farm to treat us. He recognized our symptoms immediately. His hospital had begun receiving other local survivors in recent days. Although all the early symptoms were the same, some of the patients developed more serious complications, including severe pneumonia and paralysis. A good many of them failed to make any recovery, even after intensive treatment, and soon died. A few, primarily those from farm families who lived in our area, suffered only mild initial symptoms and began to recover quickly. It appeared clear to my Uncle Bob that an epidemic was brewing, and the most common factor among the people afflicted was that they all became infected in the weeks immediately *following* the meteor impact."

"Was that when the scientists began to investigate the meteor fragments for organic material?" Jeffrey asked inquisitively.

"Very good, but not quite. The scientists hadn't found enough confirmed meteor debris at that time to conduct any detailed analysis of the rock samples. However, at Uncle Bob's urging, they did begin collecting and testing samples of the orange scum soon after it began to appear. Since Uncle Bob had alerted them to the all the illnesses he was having to treat and his concerns that they might somehow be related to the impact, they gave him some of their samples to test in his hospital's lab.

"Petersburg Memorial Hospital was very small, so their lab had limited equipment to thoroughly analyze the samples. However, Uncle Bob was one of their best and smartest doctors. He had a lot of schooling and practical experience in biology and biochemistry. He collected some uncontaminated water and mud samples from areas of the plateau that were not immediately impacted by the meteor blast and compared them to the samples the ground zero scientists gave him. He soon found a number of natural aquatic algae plants in both samples that were common to the area. However, he discovered that many of the algae plants found in the contaminated pools from the impact zone were showing signs of mutation. That, he surmised, was the reason for the unusual color. He also discovered some proteins, amino acids, and other exotic organic compounds—the most basic building blocks of all life—in the samples collected from the impact site that he didn't recognize and couldn't identify. He advised that his findings be sent to a major research lab to conduct a more thorough analysis. His findings caused the scientists to intensify their search for fragments of the meteor and opened the door for a more detailed biological study. However, by that time, more than a month had passed from the initial explosion."

"Is that what made you sick, Grandpa?"

"Not directly. Uncle Bob treated my dad and me for two or three weeks, while he was analyzing the algae and water samples. That's how we learned about it.  He also took some samples of our blood and the infection from our cuts and analyzed them.  He told us that the virus and bacteria he found in our samples were similar to common varieties, but also appeared to have mutated slightly.  He couldn't tell us any more than that.

"Within days after Dad and I became ill, the rest of our family began to show similar symptoms and eventually became sick as well.  Uncle Bob treated us all as best he could for weeks until we began to recover.  We all survived, as did most of the local people who became infected in the first few weeks after the impact.  He told us that our survival could be credited to our strong natural immune systems.  He knew that eating fresh, natural foods and doing a lot of manual labor helped strengthen our natural immune systems, which are our best weapons against the germs, bacteria, and viruses that can make us sick or kill us.  He realized that a strong immune system not only makes us immune to reinfection from most common pathogens, it also makes our bodies more resilient and better prepared to combat new contagions.  His views on the subject would be reinforced by the patterns he saw, as the illnesses began to spread."

By this point in the tale, Jeffrey had become so engrossed with the developing story that he had given up fishing for the morning.  He had reeled in his line and leaned the pole against a boulder.  I continued to fish and soon filled our bucket with enough mature trout to feed us all for supper.  However, none of them were even close to the size of my initial catch.  The intensity of his Jeffrey's stare urged me on.

"Did they eventually identify an alien life form?"  He asked.

"I'm really not sure.  Uncle Bob told us what he knew, but it was only bits and pieces.  He never actually said they discovered any living alien organisms in the debris, but he couldn't be sure how well the few confirmed samples they did find represented what was in all of the meteor debris.  Everything that happened after the impact certainly suggests some tiny alien microbes did survive the impact.  He did say that the national lab soon confirmed his findings that the scum contained exotic proteins, amino acids, and organic compounds that they had never seen before. He said they also found traces of DNA, which is the most basic genetic code for every living thing on Earth.

"DNA is a specific type of organic compound that binds with proteins and other basic compounds to make life. It tells scientists how all life forms on Earth are related to one another, even though we are not all closely related. He also told us that the organic elements and compounds they found in the debris were quickly combining with the simplest microscopic organisms that typically thrived at the impact site and were causing them to mutate quickly into new, and in some cases, more complex microorganisms.

"I know this is difficult information to understand, but Uncle Bob explained it to us this way. He had learned that a few species of animals have very different blood than people do. Most of them live in the water, like the crawdads you've found in the creek. Some of them are spiders and insects that you've seen around our farm. Although their bodies contain DNA like ours, their blood is based on copper. Ours is based on iron. Have you ever noticed what you see when you step on a spider?"

"Yes, I see a squashed spider and a lot of sticky goo."

"Well, that clear fluid that you call goo is its blood. Our blood, and the blood of all our animals is red. Uncle Bob taught us that the blood of crawdads, spiders, and other species that lived on the Earth long before we did is composed from copper. In fact, if you ever killed a crawdad, you'd see that its blood soon turns blue after it has been exposed to air. Your spider blood might do so, too, if you could watch it for a while. It's the iron in our blood that makes it red. "

"Okay, Grandpa. If all animals have the same DNA, then why do some have copper blood while we have iron blood?"

"Well, I didn't really say that we all have the *same* DNA. As I understand it from what Uncle Bob taught me, all living organisms on our planet have DNA and RNA; it's just that DNA is a complex compound that can mutate, and those mutations make each life form that is built from it distinct. Uncle Bob taught me that we don't actually know what caused the blood of humans to be different from crawdads and spiders. They lived on this planet long before we did, so whatever actually caused that mutation to occur happened before any of us could be there to see it. He said it might have occurred naturally from DNA that mutated through natural reproduction, perhaps in response to pathogens or pressure from changes in the environment. However, he told us that some people speculated that the mutation may have occurred from contamination by organic materials or microbes that came to the Earth from a meteor, like the one that fell in our area sixty years ago. It was well known that asteroids and comets had collided with Earth throughout time because the remains of many ancient impact craters have been found—some large and some small.

"As far as scientists from that time could determine, most of the species that have copper blood arose on Earth around the same point in time, perhaps sharing a common ancestral species. If that's true, then the same effect we saw from our meteor could have been triggered by an earlier meteor impact that fell to Earth eons ago. Uncle Bob said that what he was seeing happen to the microbes in the samples he analyzed from the impact zone made him think we might be witnessing the same kind of genetic mutation occur in *our* time. Since all the initial illnesses occurred immediately after the impact, he was very concerned we were facing a potential epidemic that would have dramatic effects on life as we knew it. Not only could millions of people die from it over time, but we may see genetic mutations occur that, in future generations, could alter many other common life forms in ways neither he nor anyone else could predict.

"Many others who worked at the major labs were thinking along those lines, but they wouldn't say so publicly. They didn't want to cause a global panic based solely on their unproven theories or educated guesses. Most people wouldn't understand it all, anyway. People at that time were too focused on their own daily lives to bother trying to understand a lot of scientific jargon they were never taught.  Our society had become too dependent on professional specialists, like Uncle Bob, to worry about all those complex scientific issues.  All they would tell the public was that debris from the meteor was causing some natural organisms to mutate, and that people were becoming sick from them.  The rest of the details were being held back by government officials and scientists as they struggled to decide how to control and combat it.  That would take even more time—time they really didn't have."

"Did Uncle Bob tell you how they were going to fight it?"

"He really wasn't sure they could.  He guessed they would eventually discover a drug or vaccine that could treat it (if they had enough time), but he knew that wouldn't, in and of itself, eradicate the alien organism from the natural environment.  It would just help protect people from becoming sick from it and give our human immune systems a chance to develop an immunity to it.  Given enough time, the alien microbes could even mutate into forms the vaccine couldn't treat or that might cause other pathogens to mutate.  If the alien microbes couldn't be eradicated before they could spread away from the impact site, they'd quickly be assimilated into our environment.  Uncle Bob believed that the natural assimilation process had already become unstoppable within the first month after the impact.

"Uncle Bob also told us that, before genetic engineers could even *begin* experimenting to develop a way to kill or control it, they had to learn more about the composition and structure of the alien DNA and its associated organic compounds.  All of the antibiotics, vaccines, and sanitizers we had invented in those days were designed to kill known earthborn microbes. These alien microbes came from a different solar system.  Scientists had no way to know how their modern treatments would affect the alien microbes or any earthborn organisms that had incorporated alien DNA.  They might effectively kill the new pathogens, or they might cause them to become even more deadly and resistant to treatment over time.

"Uncle Bob said any effort to kill these microorganisms would depend on whether or not the 'genome' of the microbes was stable or unstable. I didn't know what a genome was, but he told me it meant that if the alien DNA was stable, it wouldn't mutate rapidly into other forms. That might make it easier to kill with the right treatment. However, if it proved to be unstable, that meant the microbes could mutate quickly, and any attempt to aggressively attack them might cause them to develop a natural resistance to the treatment and/or mutate into deadlier forms in subsequent generations. Scientists later concluded that the mutated genome was unstable. At that point, a widespread genetic disaster was inevitable.

"Uncle Bob taught us that many of the so-called earthborn super-bugs that emerged in the decades prior to the meteor had mutated from less lethal natural organisms because they could reproduce into drug-resistant forms faster than scientists could develop new and stronger treatments to eradicate them. Uncle Bob referred to this effect as 'inverse engineering.' What he meant was that all our well-intentioned efforts to develop stronger and stronger drugs to kill and eradicate common microscopic pathogens only had the opposite effect of making them mutate into stronger and deadlier forms.

"Uncle Bob was also raised on our farm, so he had learned from his childhood experiences that you have to live with nature on its own terms. Nature is so complex and powerful that it can always find a way to keep life in a delicate balance, even if it takes many thousands of years to do so. All life forms compete with one another, but there's a limit to how far any one of them can dominate its competitors or deplete its own source of food without, sooner or later, impacting or killing itself—often by killing off its own food chain, altering the environmental conditions that sustain it, or creating a new environmental niche that allows an unforeseen competitor to eventually displace it.

"Uncle Bob always said that we were all born with the best natural defense system we could have to maintain our place within that balance—our human immune system. It doesn't save us all, but it saves enough of us to extend the survival of our species. He knew that modern science couldn't create anything to do a better job of protecting us than that, and nature would eventually find a way to fight any attempt to do so. That's why he promoted healthy living and hard work to challenge and strengthen our natural immune systems rather than trying frantically to create ever stronger drugs and antibiotics to kill harmful pathogens, only to end up making *them* stronger and more deadly. If we eat natural foods that contain the antibodies, proteins, and vitamins that will strengthen our own immune systems and we live active lifestyles that make our bodies stronger, we will build the best defense nature can provide to protect us from harmful pathogens and preserve the overall balance of life in the natural world. Sure, some people will die from those pathogens, even if they do *everything* that they should to strengthen their immune systems. But everyone will inevitably die of something sooner or later. That's the nature of life, and we can never avoid that fate.

"Humans will always have an impact on the environment, just as every other species does. Uncle Bob always pointed out that even the staunchest, most conscientious environmentalist owns and uses a waste basket. We just shouldn't delude ourselves into believing that we can live separate and apart from nature or that we can casually or arbitrarily reengineer it to suit our own needs. If none of us ever died, there wouldn't be enough food to feed us all, and we'd destabilize the balance of life on the planet to the point where *all* life could collapse. After all, except for a very few natural minerals like salt, *everything* we eat to survive was once a living organism and everything we poop contains pathogens that can make us sick."

Jeffrey chuckled at that statement. "Yes, Grandpa, even I know that. I sure do get sick of cleaning up all the goat poops in the barn every morning."

I laughed in reply. "That's a good one, Jeffrey, but that wasn't quite what I meant to say."

"I know, Grandpa, but I sure would like to pass that chore on to Johnny."

"Well, if you decide you are ready to do a new chore that he can't yet do, I'm sure your dad would consider that. When you live on a farm like we do, we all have to do our part. Farm chores never get done by themselves, although at my age, I often wish they could. That's part of the reason why we're fishing here today. Just consider it our day off for good behavior."

# 5. Pandemic

Having reached a breaking point in the story, I decided it was time to get up and stretch my legs. We had been sitting down for far too long. I suggested to Jeffrey that this would be a good time to put away our fishing gear and break into the lunch basket Laura had packed for us. We admired the beauty of the river and canyon, as we devoured our meal. It's amazing how hungry you can get when you're fishing. We talked about our catch, and I showed Jeffrey how to skip rocks on the pool we had fished.

As we finished the meal, I decided to give Prince my apple. I thought he might like a sweet treat after all the grass and wildflowers he had already eaten. Then I suggested we go for a walk along the river and continue our conversation. For a time, we just soaked in the beauty and fragrant scent of the phlox, wild mustard, and other early spring wildflowers that lined the crumbling path that once was Smoke Hole Road. It was Jeffrey who first broke the silence, as he kicked a stone at his feet.

"I was just thinking about the alien organism, Grandpa. If they couldn't kill it, what did they do about it?"

"They didn't just give up their efforts to find a treatment to kill it. They were far too smugly overconfident in their skills to do that. They were also motivated by their fears of the deadly world-wide pandemic they would eventually face. All the politicians demanded a treatment to relieve the growing public fear that the alien organism would kill them all. Uncle Bob kept advising them not to let desperation drive their search for a treatment. As he said to us many times, 'A rush to a solution is a rush to judgment with the added potential for unintended consequences we may later regret.'

"People at that time were far too egotistical about their self-professed technological superiority to view themselves as just another simple life form. Reality for them could be whatever they envisioned it to be. They just weren't able to accept death as a price for life. Actually, I don't think the fear and hysteria that arose over time was driven as much by some vague fear that many people could die as it was by the self-preservationist thought that they, themselves, would die. The global pandemonium that would eventually consume the modern society they had built seemed to be driven by a very personal fear that shattered their false sense of control over their lives and destiny. People had lived with a sense of overconfidence for so long that it became a difficult—if not impossible—adjustment for them to make.

"As you now realize, all their efforts to combat and kill the alien virus eventually failed. It just took too long to understand what they were fighting, and every desperate attempt they made to develop a treatment only proved that the organism's genome was unstable, resulting in even more variants. Some of the labs that made the attempt actually created the deadlier pathogens that Uncle Bob had warned against and caused viral outbreaks in several major cities around the world. Once they were unleashed, they could not be controlled and quickly killed millions of people who lived far away from the impact site. Even some of the scientists working in those labs contracted some form of the virus and died despite all the precautions they had taken to protect themselves and their work environment.

"However, the first transmission of the pathogen occurred in the cities and towns surrounding the impact site. Some of the first illnesses, like the one our family survived, were caused by all the ash fallout from the original explosion. As the cloud of debris radiated out in all directions from ground zero, people were exposed to the alien microbes in the dust. In turn, they reacted with common microbes in perspiration and infected cuts, like mine. Research also documented that the alien microbes were so infectious that they could even be transmitted from person to person through the air.

"In addition, the initial explosion spread contaminated dust and debris across the Eastern Continental Divide on the Allegheny Plateau. The Divide is the watershed boundary where any rain that falls to the east of it eventually drains into Atlantic Ocean via the Potomac River, the James River and their various tributaries, and rain that falls to the west drains into the Gulf of Mexico via the Mississippi River system. The source waters for these river systems were directly contaminated and quickly transmitted the alien microbes to more distant downstream cities and population centers, like Pittsburgh, Cincinnati, Louisville, Memphis, Washington, Richmond and Norfolk, during the first two-to-three weeks of the incident.  Many cities and towns drew water from these major rivers to provide drinking water to their citizens.  Although the water was treated, the treatment systems proved to be ineffective to kill the alien microbe and, in some cases, actually provided another impetus for genetic mutation.  At this early point in time, the damage was done, and there was no effective way to contain it.

"Over time, we heard news about incredible and gruesome reports of sicknesses and death.  Those who contracted the pathogen earliest and had the strongest natural immune systems were the lucky ones.  The alien pathogen remained in its earliest form during those initial days following the impact, and those of us with strong immune systems were able to survive it.  Uncle Bob said that the initial exposure we received allowed us to develop an immunity to the alien virus before it mutated into other forms.  Our overall health and that early immunity is what may have protected us from many of the deadlier forms that emerged later.  We'll never know for sure.  All I can say is that I'm still here to tell you the story.  That's all the evidence I need.

"However, the people who lived in the cities were far less healthy than any of us.  They lived comparatively sedate lives, where they did most of their daily work from a chair and lounged around in their homes after their work was done.  They ate a lot of processed foods that contained artificial additives that made it taste better (so people would buy more of it) but did little or nothing to strengthen their immune systems.

"For example, milk—the first and most basic food that all newborn mammals need to build up their underdeveloped immune systems—that most people bought from a store and drank was pasteurized.  Pasteurization is a process by which the milk is heated to a temperature that will kill all the potentially harmful germs and bacteria it may contain.  The theory is that killing those germs and bacteria will make the milk safer to consume and prevent human illness. It does effectively kill potentially harmful pathogens that may be present in fresh milk and effectively extends its shelf life. However, the pasteurization and homogenization process also indiscriminately kills all of the good bacteria and can remove proteins and antibodies that we need to strengthen our immune systems. Even many of the bad pathogens, at the low levels that they may occur naturally in fresh milk, help our systems develop a natural immunity to them early in life. People also didn't understand that the antibodies present in fresh milk will, over the first day or two after the milking, attack and naturally reduce the concentration of potentially harmful pathogens in the milk. That's why we keep the milk our goats produce cooled in the cold cellar for one day before we drink it.

"The point I'm making is that the vast majority of the people who lived away from farms ate foods that were less natural and lived lives that were less healthy, which caused them to have weaker immune systems at a time when they *needed* strong, fully developed immune systems to protect them from the alien microbes. That general condition, in turn, made government and health officials even more desperate to create a drug or vaccine that would kill the alien virus, which only made it mutate more quickly into deadlier forms. It was a fatal policy mistake driven by their unshakable belief that science can do a better job of protecting human lives than nature can.

"While their approach did have the potential to save *some* people from dying from specific common diseases that might otherwise have killed them, it also had the unintended effect of preventing nature from keeping our population in proper balance with all the other living organisms that the Earth's ecosystem must support. In other words, our efforts to save *some* human victims from death had the ultimate effect of disrupting the delicate natural balance of life. Over time, the disruption of that natural balance then contributed to a human population explosion that threatened the ability of the planet to support all life forms. Our sense of technological superiority only served to feed a belief that our lives are somehow more important to save than the lives of lesser organisms that our unnatural growth rate ultimately threatens.  I guess that's why vanity is considered to be one of the seven deadly sins.

"What's more, government and health officials couldn't say they had no way to understand the true nature of natural immunity.  They had *plenty* of historic pandemics to draw upon (although I'm sure they would claim they never realized it).  There were waves of deadly plagues on the other side of the Atlantic Ocean around 800 years before the impact.  One of the deadliest of these periodic plagues, Bubonic Plague, was caused by a bacterium in fleas that lived on mice and rats.  There were no treatments during those outbreaks because they had no knowledge of modern medicine.  By the time the humans of that era developed a natural immunity to the plague, only about one third of the population survived.  Another widespread deadly scourge was caused by the smallpox virus which killed about one third of its victims.  Repeated smallpox epidemics occurred throughout Europe over the centuries.  Those survivors who managed to develop an immunity to the disease carried the deadly virus to our country, when it was first settled by Europeans.  The Native Americans who lived here when they arrived had never been exposed to smallpox, so they had no natural immunity to it.  Many of them soon contracted the disease, and their population was decimated before they, too, developed a natural immunity.  By the time that occurred, smallpox had become the most widespread killer of Native Americans.

"Yet another deadly viral outbreak occurred in the aftermath of the first global war in 1918 and 1919.  It was called the Spanish Flu, and it killed an estimated 500 million people, which was roughly one-third of the world's total population at that time.  The last major global pandemic occurred 100 years later in 2019 and 2020.  It was a Coronavirus that killed millions of people before a vaccine was created to control its spread.  My dad and Uncle Bob lived through that pandemic and remembered it well.  They talked about all the panic that arose from that disease.  It became so great that governments across the world basically shut down their economies which eventually resulted in a severe global economic recession.  The vaccines that they developed may have controlled the spread of the virus, but the resulting economic recession caused many people to starve in its wake. It's impossible to say if the combined death toll was worse than it would have been if the virus had been allowed to run its natural course, as so many others before it had done. This historic pattern of periodic contagions can be viewed as nature's way of keeping our population in check and preventing it from spiraling out of control. People, however, reacted to them as if they were periodic wars that we had to win to maintain our ego-driven position of dominance over all other life forms.

"I believe that nature defines the ground rules that we must live by and, sooner or later, one way or another, it will always win. You have to think carefully about your perspective before you take actions that can impact the fundamental nature of life. In other words, how hard do you have to be kicked in the head by reality to learn the lesson nature is trying to teach you? When you live as close to the land and farm as we do, you learn that you have to understand and work cooperatively with nature or you risk failure. If we ask more of our land than it can support or produce, our crops will fail. Most city people never seemed to get that fundamental message, and they inevitably paid the price."

"I think I understand. What kind of sickness did the alien virus cause?" Jeffrey interjected.

"I don't know the full range of the infections, and I really didn't want to. Some of the more horrific effects we did hear about were frightening to think about. In most cases, the virus attacked the brain and the nervous system. It became, in effect, a brain-eating bacterium that made people hysterical and insane. Waves of violence erupted in the larger cities when infections spiked. Those people with advanced stages of the infection would aggressively attack other people convinced that they were protecting themselves from being killed. Others were paralyzed to the point that they couldn't breathe and ultimately suffocated to death. Skin lesions were reported in many cases that disfigured faces and hands making the victims, in extreme cases, completely unrecognizable to their own relatives. Newborn infants, if they survived to be born at all, coughed up blood and bile accumulated during their time in the womb and died within hours after birth. I could describe a lot of gruesome images that people witnessed during that time, but I think you can get the picture.

"Whenever an outbreak occurred, whole cities were quarantined and people were forced to stay in their homes. Governments reacted even more strongly than they had during the earlier Coronavirus pandemic. Virtually all businesses and industries were closed, and a form of martial law was imposed, where armed military and police officers patrolled the cities and towns arresting people who violated the curfews and quarantines. Some healthy people were shot and killed by the enforcing officers because they were so gripped by their hysterical fears that the officers couldn't tell them apart from the brain-infected victims. It was assumed that these extreme measures would reduce social interactions and control the spread of the virus. However, it lasted for such a long time that it only contributed to people's sense of fear and desperation.

"However, the measures had limited effect. They may have *slowed* the spread, but they couldn't effectively stop it. As I pointed out, a number of large public water systems in our country eventually became contaminated. Average citizens who were forced to have basic food and supplies delivered to their homes became contaminated when they opened the boxes or touched the items they had ordered. Desperate people who could not get the essential supplies they needed to survive broke into the homes of their neighbors to steal them.

"Governments tried to give citizens money to purchase the basic supplies they needed after they lost their jobs and income. However, many of those governments and countries were still trying to rebuild their depleted finances and economies from the Coronavirus pandemic that had occurred less than twenty years earlier. Their measures to control transmission of the disease and distribute financial aid to their citizens only worsened the economic impact of the disease by causing national bankruptcies and economic collapse.

Some desperate governments simply printed more valueless money that just eroded the buying power of their currency.  That only caused runaway inflation when people had to pay more money for the products they bought because the purchasing power of their money declined.  In some cases, consumer prices rose over one hundred percent in a single day.

"People in many nations were ready to revolt against their governments. Eventually, government officials blamed other nations for their plight as a way to channel and deflect the anger of their citizens.  Nations that produced fuel for all the automobiles and trucks around the world eventually stopped selling it because they couldn't get the price that they demanded for it, and they decided they could use it as a bargaining chip for protection from other countries.  Border wars and skirmishes between nations began to erupt, which only expanded the death toll and the destruction that was being wrought internally by infected victims and roving bands of desperate survivors. Ultimately, the modern society was coming apart at the seams.  The final downfall had begun."

With that statement, Jeffrey and I had returned to our fishing site.  Prince was waiting patiently for us with the shay.  He greeted us with a boisterous whinny, as if to demand an explanation for why we had left him behind for so long.  It was now the early afternoon and the time had come for us to return home.  We killed the rest of the fish we had caught, mounted them on our string line, and refilled the bucket with fresh water from the stream.  We put the fish in the bucket as best as we could to keep them cool on the trip home. We would clean and fillet them after we returned.  Finally, we took our seats on the shay and, with a gentle snap of the reins and a stern "giddy-up" command to Prince, we began the journey home.

# 6. Endgame

For the first ten or so minutes of our ride, Jeffrey was quiet. I could tell he was mulling over in his mind everything I had told him. I thought maybe he'd heard enough for the day, until he finally looked over at me and asked another question.

"Grandpa, did you ever find out how many people survived?"

"Not really, Jeffrey. We stayed close to our home and avoided all the cities. There wasn't anything we could do to stop all the destruction, so we decided to take care of ourselves. At least doing that wouldn't make it worse for the people struggling to survive in the outside world.

"Within the first few years after the meteor impact, we started to see some bedraggled survivors wandering along the Petersburg Pike, slowly working their way through the mountains. They were starving and desperate. Many of them had scars on their faces, hands, and legs that made us realize they were among the few to recover from the alien microbe. Virtually all of them asked for our help. We did what we could, but there were just too many of them, and we couldn't produce enough food to feed them all. As I said earlier, the number of stragglers gradually decreased over time until they came no more. That's when we decided it was finally over. Perhaps a few of the most remote, isolated cities survived, but if they did, we never heard about it.

"However, one day, during the third year following the impact, a man and a woman with a sixteen-year-old daughter stopped at our farm. All of them were covered with scars from the pathogen, but they had managed to survive. Their clothes were dirty, ragged, and torn. The man told us they had come from Washington, DC where they had lived for years, although they were born and raised in eastern Kentucky. He had worked for the government as the chief of staff for a prominent senator. They hid at their home in suburban Virginia until all the looting and pillaging ended and then left to seek a new life away from all the death and destruction. They had used their money to stockpile food and supplies in their basement when they understood what was going to happen. They stayed hidden in their home until their supplies were exhausted.

"His wife suffered from anxiety attacks caused by the nightmarish horrors she had experienced during their confinement. At one point, he had to rescue her from a man driven insane by the alien virus who tried to rape and murder her. Her husband managed to kill the invader before he had a chance to kill her. That was the person who had given them the virus.

"We let them stay with us for several months while they recovered from severe malnutrition. They were very nice people, and they did their best to help us improve and work the farm. They had some basic farming experience from their upbringing in Kentucky. The man told us many stories of the horrors they suffered in Washington. I remember some of them, but I don't think it would be right to burden you with the worst of them. Those I will take to my grave.

"He did tell me about all the destruction that occurred in Washington. While most of the federal government buildings remained standing, they had been severely damaged by protestors and rioters who smashed many of the windows and ravaged the interiors. While they couldn't burn the concrete and stone exteriors of the buildings, they did firebomb the wooden interiors, and sooty scorch marks around the exterior windows of many buildings revealed the extent of the damage. Many of the row houses and homes in the surrounding residential areas were destroyed from intentional burnings and natural wildfires that raged unchecked throughout the city. Government officials would not allow firefighters to spray public water on the fires for fear that it might spread the contamination. All they could do was build fire lines around the burning buildings in the hope that they could contain them from spreading. As conditions continued to deteriorate, there weren't enough firefighters left to combat the growing number of fires. According to his estimates, more than two-thirds of the city's neighborhoods eventually burned to the ground.

"Conditions in the outlying areas where he lived were no less devastating. Most of the homes in his own suburban neighborhood also had been burned. During one mass riot that struck his community, he had to protect his own home from burning when two of his neighbor's homes caught fire. He stood outside all throughout the night spraying it with a garden hose every time windblown embers landed on his house. He had no fear of using public water at the time because he and his family had already been infected by the virus. After the riot, virtually all of the remaining survivors walked away aimlessly because they couldn't survive any longer in the devastated remains. They all abandoned their homes to search for food and shelter far beyond the city in response to desperate rumors about places in the countryside that were untouched by the disaster. Less than six months later, his family would follow them.

"Throughout their entire five-week walking journey to our farm, they encountered only a few scattered survivors. Many of them were lone stragglers wandering aimlessly in search of food. They encountered a few surviving rural families, like us, who were still eking out a marginal life on their farms. Most of them greeted his family with guns, because they had been forced to defend their food and supplies from desperate roaming gangs. Some people they met noticed the scars they bore from the virus and chased them off because they feared reinfection. They barely managed to steal enough food from the gardens and fields they passed until they could find more sympathetic families to take them in and give them rest. Given the condition they were in by the time they reached our farm, I honestly believe they wouldn't have survived another day of travel had we not offered them food and shelter.

"After a few months of intensive care and recovery from us, the man and his wife decided they needed to continue their desperate journey. They couldn't live without knowing what ultimately happened to all of their family in Kentucky. Just the thought that they might be struggling to survive without them tormented his wife. Family ties mean as much to rural people who live in Kentucky as they do to us here in West Virginia. As the time for their departure drew near, the man had only one request of us. He asked if we would please keep his daughter with us until they could return for her. The rigors of the journey into the mountains were very hard on her, and they knew their chances of surviving the trip would be better if they had one less mouth to feed. They trusted us to do this favor for them because they knew we would care for her as one of our own. If they did have to face death along the way, he knew it would be a comfort for his wife to know that her daughter would continue to live safely in the supporting embrace of our family. My parents were touched by his request and eagerly consented.

"Many tears were shed on the day our visitors departed. Their daughter suffered emotional distress for weeks. My heart ached and reached out to her. All that she had left behind to remember her parents and her former life were a few scraps of papers, postcards, and tokens in an old shoebox—the very items I showed you last night. Another two years later, I asked her to marry me, and she became your great grandmother.

"She waited patiently and eagerly for years, but her parents never returned. Only once did she suggest that we go to search for them, but I never knew where in Kentucky they were from, and she couldn't remember the name of the town. Any attempt we could have made to search for them would have been dangerous and futile. We will never know if they survived or not.

"It was a horrible time of death and destruction that lasted at least five long years from the day of the impact. It truly brought out the best and worst of human behavior. It seemed there was little in between. We never really heard any estimates of how many people were left. I would guess that the alien virus and the disaster that was wrought in its aftermath eventually killed over seven billion people. We don't even know if any of the former governments survived, but I would doubt it. All we know for sure is that there is no one left here to tell us what we can or cannot do.

"I suppose there could be many millions of lucky survivors scattered around the world or there could be only a few hundred thousand. I have no reason to believe there would be any more than that. I suppose we could have ventured out to see what actually happened in some of the nearest cities to us, but seeing all the devastation for ourselves wouldn't have made it any easier to comprehend or to accept. There simply comes a time when you have to carry on with your life and let the past remain where it belongs. Life goes on. As long as we remember the lessons the great cataclysm taught us, we can know that whatever future we work hard to build will be better. The life you have with us on this farm is all the proof of that I need to see."

I turned my head to Jeffrey and noticed a tear forming in his eye. He now knew the full depth and magnitude of the secrets of that time that I harbored in my memory. I could tell he understood why I hadn't told him about it before. For him, the tale became what I call a 'terminal reality.' It's a time when one understanding you may have of the world comes to an abrupt end and you are faced with a whole new reality—not unlike the struggles faced by Native Americans when they met the first Europeans and realized that their whole understanding of the world and their place within it had suddenly and irrevocably changed.

I had just given Jeffrey an entirely new understanding of the world we live in, and I knew it would take time for him to fully comprehend its meaning. I let him mull it over quietly in his mind for the rest of the journey home, while I enjoyed the lilting sounds of the birds, the scent of the spring wildflowers that drifted with the breeze, and the captivating beauty of the forested mountains in the distance.

# 7. Life's Little Lessons

Jeffrey's dad was the first person to greet us when we arrived at the farm. He was quite impressed by all the fish we caught and Jeffrey's animated tale of the eighteen-pound whopper. After we retrieved all our supplies from the shay, Matthew led Prince back to the barn, where he unhitched and stored the rig, removed the harness, and bedded him down for the evening. Jeffrey helped me carry our equipment back to the farmhouse, where Kelly and Laura were preparing to cook our supper.

"Now, I don't even want to *see* the fish in that bucket until you've scaled, cleaned, and filleted them!" Laura admonished. "You're not going to mess up our kitchen while we're getting ready for supper. The two of you can just take those fish over to the cabin and finish up. Just make sure you get them ready for us soon, or you'll go to bed with an empty belly."

Jeffrey and I sheepishly retreated to my cabin and broke out the fish scaler and a sharp knife from the tackle box. We poured the water out of the bucket and set up our fish processing operation on the open porch. I told Jeffrey to scale the fish, and I would fillet them. We put all the remains in the bucket so we could dump them in the ravine when we were done. By then, Jeffrey had been given some time to digest the tale of the great disaster.

"Thank you for telling me the story, Grandpa. It's just hard for me to understand why the survivors didn't try to rebuild their cities like we rebuilt our farm. After all, if that's the only life they knew and understood, didn't they want to get it back?"

"Oh, I'm sure the vast majority of them would have given anything to have their old lives back. You could sense it in the despair of many survivors we encountered in the end times. But you have to remember, most of those people were trained and educated to do specialized skills. They didn't have the broad base of knowledge it would take to know how to rebuild the cities or the technology they had become so dependent upon. That's why we make sure everyone on the farm knows how to do all the chores. If one of us gets ill or injured, someone else knows how to step in and take over. Those people had such specialized skills that they could do a highly technical job, but they didn't know how to fix a sandwich.

"You also have to remember that all the businesses that mass-produced the machines, food, and buildings they depended upon were shut down and stopped producing them. They might have been able to salvage some of the materials and equipment they needed to begin rebuilding, but that wouldn't last for long. With all the extensive damage that occurred, they probably would have run out of supplies long before they completed the task. When our farm was severely damaged, we had to comb through a lot of abandoned and destroyed farms and buildings throughout our valley to salvage some of the materials we needed. Rebuilding a city is a much more complex, labor-intensive and time-consuming job than rebuilding our farm. In many cases, we relied upon our ingenuity to find a way to make do with what we had. City people weren't accustomed to 'making do.' They relied upon their money to buy what they needed, and now that was gone or worthless.

"I guess I think of their technologically-advanced society—and perhaps all of nature—as a spinning top. Once you get it spinning, it's amazing and elegant to watch. Balanced delicately on a tiny point, it spins so effortlessly and with such stability for so long that it makes you believe it will spin forever. However, the slightest nudge makes it wobble erratically until it finally falls. Once it does, it just lays there until you start it all over again. As complex as their society had become before it finally fell, they probably couldn't even conceive of how to begin starting it all over again.

"While the survivors probably could have banded together to do the job, you also have to remember that most of them had become desperate to feed and protect themselves. Once their society had collapsed into chaos, it was hard for people to trust desperate strangers enough to invest their energy in such a major cooperative project. We had a large family that cared for one another and knew we had to work together to survive. That's the only way you can survive on a farm. The work is hard, and you may not succeed, but you *know* you will fail if you don't make the effort. Although city people were highly dependent on their technology and people with specialized skills, they were far too concerned about their own immediate survival to marshal what few people they had left. I guess it was easier and more practical to search for their needs elsewhere than to worry about rebuilding the cities."

"Didn't they have *any* faith in their ability to figure out how to do it? Why didn't they pray for guidance?" Jeffrey inquired.

"That's another good question. I really don't know if I can answer that one. Faith had become a difficult concept for the people who lived in the modern society. They had lived successfully for so many generations with all their advanced technology and modern conveniences, that they couldn't even conceive of life without them. They looked at our self-reliant lifestyle as if it was regressive, outdated, or quaint. They felt they had advanced far beyond that and no longer needed to live that way. They were so glibly proud of their technological superiority that they no longer felt that they needed to rely upon faith. Their confidence in their technological superiority became a faith of its own. To them, science would eventually find an answer to any questions they had, and nothing was beyond human understanding. The allure and power of all their wealth, labor-saving devices, and advanced technology encouraged them to believe that modern society would eventually provide the answers to all their questions and solve all of their problems. Yet, when the meteor struck, their glittering modern society left them only with destruction, despair, and hopelessness. I would hope that the disaster eventually made them understand that they were wrong. But that realization, if it occurred at all, was too little, too late to help them.

"Public opinion surveys taken during those times showed that urban people were turning away from religion. Many of them would bristle at the mention of the words, 'faith' or 'God.' What they didn't seem to understand is that 'faith' is a basic part of the human conscience. As it has been defined, 'faith' is a belief in things that are unknown or can never be known. Even the greatest scientists of the modern world discovered that every question they studied about the nature of the universe only raised more questions they couldn't answer. The universe is unimaginably big and complex. Even trying to understand and grasp how nature works on our own tiny world is mind-boggling. Many times, we only learn how it really works when we've made a mistake and have to live with the consequences, as the story I just told you illustrates.

"People gradually accepted the belief that life exists on other planets because it was too hard to accept that we could be the only intelligent life in a universe as vast as ours with so many distant worlds. I agree that's a reasonable, rational way to look at it. I guess they didn't stop to think that it is just as difficult to conceive that a universe as big, complex, diverse, and elegantly conducive to life as ours could arise completely by chance, as though it was the *only* possible outcome. Certainly, the complex machines they built didn't invent or build themselves, and life is far more complex and far more difficult to create than any of them were.

"When you get right down to the bare essence of the human conscience, it's clear that *all* people rely on faith to allay their fears of the unknown, often far more that they realize or wish to admit. Even people who refuse to believe in God or religion have to rely on their faith that there is no God. After all, they can't *prove* that God doesn't exist any more definitively than a believer can prove that He does.

"Scientists of the time created complex models to test their theories of how nature and the universe worked. Many of them *insisted* that the results of their models could not be questioned because they were based on rigorous or 'hard science.' However, their complex models typically relied upon a number of critical assumptions about certain aspects of nature that even they didn't fully understand or couldn't accurately or reliably quantify. Consequently, their models were ultimately influenced by their own faith about how critical elements of nature worked, even though they couldn't prove those assumptions were correct. Perhaps that's why so many of their models didn't produce the exact same results even when they were modeling the same thing.  In many cases, their models had to be adjusted (recalibrated) just to be able to predict what we already know to be real or what we actually see in the natural world.  Regardless of what people say or want to think, everyone ultimately relies on his own personal faith to give meaning and understanding to his life.

"All I can say about faith is that no one can tell you what you should or should not believe about things that cannot be known.  You will have to decide that for yourself, and you will ultimately bear the consequences for it.  However, I would warn you not to let your faith close your mind to other ways of thinking.  Your faith should help expand your understanding, not arbitrarily constrain it.  As farmers, we deal with and accept reality on its own terms.  If life tells you that your beliefs don't match what reality is trying to teach you, then you may have to make some adjustments to your faith, just as the scientists were forced to adjust their models.  If you can't do that, then you may learn that you've let your faith dictate what reality is.  That's when you will probably end up making a potentially serious error of judgment, and reality is not likely to forgive you or feel sorry for you.  It certainly didn't forgive any of us when the meteor fell."

Jeffrey pondered my words momentarily, then looked up at me.  "Does that mean you think their loss of faith made it harder for them to be hopeful about their ability to rebuild their cities?"

"Perhaps," I pondered.  "It certainly makes sense.  In my mind, it explains the despair and depression we could see written indelibly in the faces of the survivors we met.  Faith can be a great source of comfort in times of uncertainty and adversity, and it is a source of hope when you need it most.  It can help us bridge the gap between our knowledge and the unknown in a way that inspires us to learn more.  It can be a guide to teach us how we should relate to one another and the natural world that sustains us.  When you look closely at people who casually reject the power and influence of faith on their lives, you will see the darkest depths of human fear, despair, and hopelessness.  However, it can also be a very sharp double-edged sword.  If your faith makes it impossible for you to learn what reality is trying to teach you, then you may live to regret it.

"I realize that it can be very difficult and humbling at times to accept what reality teaches us. I've had to face that so many times in my life that I can't even begin to count them all. However, you need to understand that life's adversities are not inherently good or bad. The adversities you will face in life may seem bad to you, but in the grand scheme of things, they're simply life's little lessons. They teach us how and when we need to adjust our thinking and our beliefs. If we fail to heed them and internalize them, we risk repeating our errors. That's why you can't let your faith arbitrarily dictate your entire view of the world and our place within it. There are many people who will try to manipulate your faith to serve their own personal needs. Human history has been littered with them. As long as you have confidence in your own judgment, you won't fall prey to them.

"People can convince themselves of anything. When you lose your faith in the resilience of the human spirit, you don't have much else to rely upon. That's why I believe many victims may have died from suicide. They just couldn't deal with all the uncertainty and adversity they had to face. That's when they needed faith the most. Use your reasoning and common sense, guided by your understanding of nature and reality, to decide what you should believe. You're a smart kid, and I trust you to make those decisions for yourself. After all, who knows what new lessons life will teach us today?"

Jeffrey beamed a reassuring smile in my direction. "That makes a lot of sense to me, Grandpa. It really helps me understand what happened. I'll think about it some more and talk to you if I have any more questions."

"That's what I'm here for, Jeffrey. Nothing would make me happier than to see you succeed in life. I'm glad you appreciate nature and our lives on this farm. It's a difficult, but good and healthy way to live and learn. That appreciation, and your genetic immunity to the alien virus, are the greatest gifts I can give you."

I had just finished answering Jeffrey's questions, when Paul, his youngest brother, raced up to me, panting. "Whoa there little boy, what's got you so excited?"

"Grandpa, Grandpa, you've got to come quick!" Paul implored, as he pulled on my arm and gulped air to catch his breath. "I found a big black and red spider over the door to the cold cellar. You've got to come and see it!"

"Okay, Paul. We just need to finish cleaning the fish for supper. Why don't you go ask your dad to look at it first, and I'll be right along in a couple of minutes."

"I did, I did!" Paul exclaimed. "Dad saw it and told me to go find you, quick."

"Why? What's the big rush?"

"Dad wants you to come and see it right away. The spider's body is bigger than his whole hand! We found it eating a bird that it caught. Dad said it's the *biggest, nastiest*-looking spider he's ever seen!"

I glanced across the table at Jeffrey, but he was already looking back at me. His eyes were wide open.

# Part II.  *The Wilderness Expedition*

# 8. The Spider

Paul grabbed my right arm with both hands and tugged with all his might, as he excitedly urged me to follow him to the cold cellar. Knowing he was only six years old, I misjudged his strength, and he nearly pulled me out of my chair. It took all the balance I could muster to resist him.

"Paul! Stop!" I sternly implored. He released his grip. "Let me finish filleting this last fish. Your dad and the spider can wait. Jeffrey, would you please collect up all the trout fillets and take them in to your mom. She's waiting for them. Then you can follow behind us to the cold cellar to see what this is all about. We'll clean up and dump the fish remains when we get back."

Paul's legs were short, but he could move them fast enough to challenge my ability to keep up with him. I watched him gain distance on me as his silky blond hair bounced with every step. "Hurry, Grandpa, hurry!" he cajoled, as he looked back and saw me lagging behind. The urgency he felt reflected in his voice. The thought that all of my 'hurry-up and go' got up and went many years ago never crossed his mind.

I watched him slow down, as he started to descend the concrete stairway that we had cut into the ravine bank next to the cold cellar. "Paul, be careful on those steps, and hold onto the railing!" Almost instinctively and before I could finish my command, his left hand grabbed the iron pipe railing. He had been reminded about that many times in the past.

When I reached the top of the stairway, I saw Paul and his dad standing back from the front of the cold cellar, their gaze locked in amazement at the doorway. The entryway to the cold cellar was built into the bank of the ravine. We had excavated a large storage area into the bank and lined the walls with rocks and heavy wooden pillars for stability. A series of food storage shelves lined the walls between the support pillars. A simple hip roof, a front wall and doorway, and two partial side walls emanating from the bank comprised the entranceway. Only the doorway and the roof were built of wood—the exterior walls were built entirely from chiseled stone blocks.

A perennial spring that poured from a nearby sandstone cliff just upstream from the cold cellar provided the source of clean, fresh drinking water for our farm, the house, and the cold cellar. We had piped some of the spring water into the cold cellar when we excavated it, and the line fed through a large, four-foot by eight-foot open stainless-steel tub (salvaged from a former sugar camp) that we used to keep our milk and other perishable food stores properly cooled throughout the summer. The cold spring water running through the cellar, combined with the cool, ground-insulated subterranean location and shelter from direct sunlight kept the cellar at a consistent air temperature of about 45-50 degrees throughout the year. The spring water running through the storage tub maintained a cooler temperature of about 40 degrees for the jars and crocks we stored in it. The system provided a perfect way to naturally preserve our most temperature-sensitive foods when our refrigerator and other electrical devices became useless in the wake of the great cataclysm. Ingenuity and self-reliance now powered our daily lives.

Paul had been sent by his mother to retrieve a quart jar of canned beans for supper, when he noticed the spider on a narrow ledge above the doorway into the cellar. Its large size scared him as it clambered about a dead goldfinch it had somehow killed. His scream at the sight of the spider had caught his father's attention, who rushed to see what was happening. Realizing that he had never seen such a large spider, Matthew sent Paul to find me, while he stood guard over it with a shovel he had been using at the time.

"What do you make of it?" Matthew asked me. "Have you ever seen the likes of it before?"

I was caught without an immediate answer, when my eyes first locked on it. The body of the spider was at least eight inches long, maybe longer. Its legs, when extended to walk, easily added another five to six inches in overall length. In addition to its legs, I noticed two curved fangs or pincers emanating from its head. It periodically pierced the bird's body with those fangs, as though it was trying to inject it with some form of venom to kill or paralyze it. It only stabbed at the bird when it tried to twitch one of its wings or open its beak—perhaps struggling to breathe. As the bird's death throes slowly subsided, the spider deftly climbed over and around it, as if testing to confirm that it was dead.

The spider's body appeared to be covered in a thick layer of very short fur, not unlike the tiny jumping spiders I had seen throughout my life. However, I noticed a number of bright red patches or spots all over its abdomen. If the spider was aware of our presence, it never froze or tried to escape. It acted as though it wasn't aware of us or didn't care. I got the immediate impression that it had no innate fear of us. That thought alone sent a shiver down my spine.

A crudely spun, heavy silk web built underneath the overhang peak of the roof revealed the spider's probable home or hiding place, from which it could pounce down on any unsuspecting bird or other prey that decided to rest on the ledge above the doorway. It had to move very quickly to pounce on and catch a skittish bird like that. That realization caused us to keep a good distance from it. When I suddenly became aware that Paul was slowly edging closer to get a better look at it, I placed my hand gently on his shoulder and drew him back.

"Keep away from it, Paul. I don't want you to scare it away or make it defensive. Let your dad pick you up if you want to get a better look." Matthew handed me the shovel and lifted Paul slowly into his arms. "I have to admit, Matthew, I've never seen anything like it myself."

I saw a stern look form on Matthew's face. "That's what I was afraid of, Grandpa. I knew I had never seen a spider that big before in my life, but I didn't know if it was something you had seen in the years before the meteor. What do you think we should do—kill it?"

"It doesn't pose any threat to us right now. Let's see what it's going to do with that bird and then we'll decide. I'd like to learn what I can about its behavior before we do anything rash. We can't learn if we don't observe."

At this point, Jeffrey came down the stairs to join us. I motioned to him to move slowly and quietly, so he wouldn't scare the spider. His chin dropped as his gaze caught sight of it. "Just stand still and watch with us, Jeffrey," I softly whispered to him.

We continued quietly watching the spider for several minutes, transfixed by its movements, as it probed the bird periodically with its front legs. It soon appeared to be satisfied that its prey was dead, and it slowly took a commanding position over the bird and bit down onto it with what appeared to be its mandible. I noticed some very slight, regular up and down movement of its abdomen, as it appeared to draw fluid from the bird. After a few moments, I gently nudged Matthew.

"I don't know for sure, Matthew, but I think it's draining fluid from the dead bird. Perhaps the venom it injected into it not only paralyzes it but also liquifies its internal organs so it could feed on it."

Paul simply said, "*Gross*!" and turned away to bury his face against his father's shirt. "I'm scared, Dad. I don't like it. Kill it with the shovel, Grandpa."

"Hold on another couple of minutes, Paul. We need to learn what we can about it before we just kill it. Do you want to go back to the house? You'll be safe there."

"Yes, Grandpa," Paul said in a whimpering voice. "Put me down, Dad, I want to go."

Matthew slowly lowered Paul to the ground, and he cautiously began to creep up the stairs, looking back toward us all the way. When he reached the top of the steps, he took off in a flash.

"Do you know what it is, Grandpa?" Jeffrey whispered to me.

"Well, Jeffrey, it's not a type of spider I've ever seen before. It looks a little like those tiny jumping spiders we often see, but it's much bigger than any spider I've known. I've never seen a spider hunt and catch anything as big as a bird. All the spiders I know eat insects."

Jeffrey looked up at me, and I could see fear in his eyes. "Do you think it was infected by the alien microbe?"

"I don't know what I can say about that. I certainly can't deny it, but it doesn't seem likely. Spiders do reproduce more quickly and in much larger numbers than humans, so any genetic mutation of spiders could occur in less time, but what little Uncle Bob taught me about genetics makes it hard for me to believe that such a substantial mutation could possibly occur within sixty years. He did say that he was concerned about what long-term effects the microbes could eventually have on other life forms, but I don't think he'd jump to that conclusion. Unfortunately, Uncle Bob died about thirty-five years ago, so we can't ask him about it. We need to think about this some more. That's why I want to study this one closely for now."

"Didn't you tell me just this morning that spider blood is based on copper, and that Uncle Bob thought that might have been caused by alien microbes from a meteor that fell long, long ago?" Jeffrey persisted. "Don't you think that influence might make it mutate more quickly today?"

"Uncle Bob said that was only one of several theories proposed to explain how some species ended up with copper-based blood, but it was never proven. We may never know how that occurred, but you may be thinking along the right track. It's hard to believe that there might be some genetic similarity in alien DNA delivered to Earth in meteor events separated in time by so many millions of years, but I can't casually dismiss it. It was known before the great catastrophe that numerous rocks blasted from the moon and Mars by ancient meteor impacts had eventually fallen on Earth. Who's to say that two meteors blasted from another solar system so far away couldn't fall on the Earth over a very long period of time. It seems to me that the odds against it would be huge, but not totally impossible."

"Wait a minute," Matthew implored. "What's all this about spiders and copper-based blood? I don't remember you telling me about that, Grandpa?"

"It's something Uncle Bob told me that Jeffrey and I were discussing this morning. While most complex life on Earth has iron-based blood, a few specific species, like spiders and crawdads, have blood based on copper. No one knew why, but Uncle Bob had an interest in it. He mentioned it to me long ago when he was explaining his concerns about the potential long-term genetic impacts of the alien microbe. Jeffrey was asking if that might explain why this unknown spider could emerge in such a brief span of time after the interstellar meteor impact. He may have a point, but we don't have the ability to know for sure."

"Well," Jeffrey interjected, refocusing the subject. "Mom wanted me to find out why it's taking so long to fetch a jar of green beans."

"I guess she'll figure that out from Paul," I chuckled, as I glanced over to Matthew. "I doubt she'll come out here on her own to see. She hates spiders."

Matthew smiled back at me and said guardedly, "I'll just let you handle that one, Grandpa, but I'll tell you this. If we don't go back to the house and tell Laura and Kelly that we killed it, you can expect to fetch a lot of canned goods from the cold cellar from here on out."

I knew he was right. I looked back up at the spider and noticed that it seemed to lift its head up. It worked its mandibles slightly and backed away from the bird. It then crept slowly up the wall to the silky nest it had built and crawled inside—perhaps getting ready for an after-meal nap. I decided that was all we were going to learn from this incident, so I took the shovel and jammed it into the apex of the roof. I could hear a crunching sound, as the web tore and the spider dropped down to the ground. We all jumped back away from it as it fell, and watched carefully as its long legs contracted against its body. I poked at it once, but it didn't move.

Satisfied that it was dead, I carefully scooped it up with the shovel, and we marched back to the house like a funeral procession. Matthew took a bucket out of the barn and I deposited the dead spider into it. I then dutifully went back to the cold cellar, opened the door, and retrieved a quart jar of green beans. Of course, I was careful to survey the cold cellar after my eyes adjusted to the dark. There was no evidence of any other spiders in the storage area. They were too big to crawl under the door anyway, and there was no prey in the cellar for them to eat. However, I made sure I had shut the door very tightly when I left.

# 9. The Decision

Matthew and I cleaned up all the fish remains from my cabin porch and dumped them in the ravine on the north side of our farm. We chatted for a time about the spider we found and what we should do about it. We knew that Paul would quickly spread the story to all of the children, and that the youngest children would soon have nightmares about it. Fortunately, I could trust Jeffrey not to make matters worse by telling them about the great cataclysm and the alien microbe. Fears of a giant spider would be difficult enough to deal with.

When we all sat down together for supper, an uneasy silence prevailed over the meal, until Paul finally spoke up. "Grandpa, did you see any more of those spiders in the cold cellar?"

I looked across the table at Matthew and Laura, who were seated together. They looked back at me simultaneously. "No, Paul. I checked it carefully, and I didn't see any others."

"Are you sure the one we found is dead?" he continued.

"Yes, your grandpa and I killed it." Matthew consoled. "You don't have to worry about it anymore, son."

"But what if there are more of them out in the woods?" Paul's older brother, John, and his seven-year-old sister Erin suddenly looked up as a wave of fear washed across their faces.

That was the question I didn't want to answer. Matthew and Laura looked at each other and then turned to me, as I contemplated my response. "I don't know how to answer that question, Paul. This is the only one we've ever seen. Maybe it's a straggler from way up on the mountain. I don't think there can be many of them around our farm because we've never seen them before. We spend so much time in the woods all around our farm that we'd surely know if they were there. It would be hard for spiders that big to hide from us for long. But, if they are out there somewhere in the woods, they must be afraid of us or we would have seen them before now. I'll bet the one we found just got lost, and you won't have to worry about them bothering you again."

I wasn't sure if I successfully allayed their fears, or if they could see through my false air of confidence. The truth of the matter was that I had no idea how many of them might be out there or where they came from. I just knew there couldn't be only one of them. None of Matthew's or Mike's siblings, who lived up and down the valley from us, had ever reported seeing anything like the spider we found. It was likely that it came down from Cave Mountain because the forest had fully recovered on all the high mountains to our west. We couldn't assure the children that there were no more giant spiders because we'd lose their trust if we were proven wrong. We also couldn't tell them there might be many more if we weren't sure of that, because the children would only suffer from nightmares, as Matthew's generation had over the story of the great cataclysm. This issue would be a matter for Mike, Kelly, Matthew, Laura and I to discuss further after the children were put to bed.

The rest of our meal was governed by an uncomfortable forced conversation, as we tried to divert the children's natural questions and fears about the spider. After supper, the children were sent off to finish their evening chores, as the adults cleaned up the kitchen and dishes. As usual, the work helped distract the children's minds, and as dusk began to descend over our farm, we adults gathered on the porch to watch the younger children play in the yard. Jeffrey, lost in deeper thoughts about all he had learned over the past two days, sat with us on the porch steps.

I had been watching Jeffrey mull over his thoughts for a while, when I finally spoke up and said, "I guess you've got a lot more to think about than I anticipated when I told you about the great disaster, Jeffrey." The other adults perked up and awaited Jeffrey's response with silent anticipation.

"Don't worry, Grandpa. It's nothing I can't handle. I won't talk to John, Erin, Paul or any of my cousins about it. I also know how hard it was for you to answer Paul's questions at the supper table. I sure don't know what to say about it, much less think about it. I guess the spider issue is only the tip of the iceberg. Now that we found this spider, I wonder what *else* might be out there in the woods that we haven't seen? How can we know what effects the alien microbe had?"

Laura suddenly chimed in. "Jeffrey, I think you hit the nail on the head. We simply don't know the answers to those questions. Fortunately, the other children know nothing about the alien microbe. We never really gave any attention to those questions before now because we hadn't seen anything strange enough to raise them. I think we do have to decide what we're going to do about it soon before the other children ask those questions."

Laura looked in my direction. As the only member of the family who lived before the meteor impact, I knew they would all be looking to me for answers. I was the only one who remembered how things were before the disaster, so I was the only one who could know what had changed since then. That's why Matthew wanted me to see the spider.

However, my knowledge of biology and biochemistry was very limited. I was only fifteen when the meteor fell, and I had not completed high school. Dad and Uncle Bob taught me all they could, but they had both passed away, and I couldn't get any more guidance from them. How was I going to fill in my own knowledge gap to answer these pressing questions?

"Jeffrey, we've got to talk about this some more before I can even begin to answer your questions. I'm just getting too old to have the answers on the tip of my tongue anymore. We're all going to have to put our heads together and decide what to do next. Before we can do that, I have to ask you a favor. Would you please get yourself and the other children ready for bed for us? They'll follow your lead. We can't let them overhear what we're discussing until we decide what we can say. I think you're getting smart enough to keep the younger children from getting too scared about the spider before they get to sleep. I'll be sure to tell you what we decide to do tomorrow morning. Would you do that for us?"

Jeffrey beamed at my confidence in him. He realized he was being asked to assume some responsibility—not just being sent away. He got up from the porch and called to his brothers and sister. Moments later, he was leading them all in their goodnight kisses and prodding them to get ready for bed. Kelly followed them into the house and returned with a lit lantern to provide some soft light for our discussion. She hung it from a hook on the porch ceiling. We just sat quietly for about 15 minutes while we waited for the children to settle down before we began discussing what we needed to do.

***** *****

As the evening drew quiet, the chirping of the crickets got louder. Mike eventually took the lead.

"Dad, I remember you once said that there was a library in Petersburg. Don't you think there might be some books there that would help us?"

"That's a good thought, Mike. It wasn't a big library, but they did have a lot of books. However, my dad and Uncle Bob went to that library, as well as the library in the old Petersburg High School, several years after the meteor struck. They were looking for books we could use as textbooks to homeschool me and the rest of their children. I went with them on that trip. Unfortunately, scavengers had already raided and ransacked nearly all the businesses and institutions in town looking for food, supplies, materials, money—anything of value they thought they could use to survive. When they couldn't find anything useful anymore, they burned the buildings out of anger and frustration. So much time has passed since then that I'm sure there's little left in them that hasn't been damaged by prolonged exposure to the elements.

"We did find a few useful books in the two libraries, but I doubt any of them would cover the highly technical subjects that would help us. Even so, I guess Kelly and Laura could comb through the boxes in the attic tomorrow, where we stored the remaining books that we couldn't use for homeschooling. If there are some reference books on spiders, chemistry, or biology we might be able to make use of them.

"However, even if some reference books may be helpful, I think we still have some important fundamental issues to resolve that no book can answer. First, we need to determine where the spider came from. I'm sure it's not the only one out there, and we don't know what kind of threat they might pose on down the road. I also think Jeffrey correctly identified the other important issue we need to resolve—what other changes have occurred where the meteor exploded on the Allegheny Plateau? If the appearance of this spider is somehow related to or caused by the alien microbes, it's likely that we'll find more of them on the plateau. We also may discover some other strange mutations that we haven't yet encountered. To me, those are the most immediate concerns to address before we can understand what we might be facing with this spider. We can only answer those nagging questions by exploring that area. Perhaps we should consider mounting an expedition."

"I understand, but that's not something that can be done in a day," Mike interjected. "I haven't been all the way to the plateau, but I've been far enough to know that the terrain is very rugged and the weather conditions in the high elevations can turn severe at a moment's notice—especially during spring. How can we possibly dedicate all the people, food, and horses we would need to undertake an expedition of that magnitude?"

"You're right, son. Those are important issues to consider. However, I don't think we have any choice. We either explore that area and learn what we may face in the future or face the consequences with uncertainty and fear when they catch us unprepared. We depend on our livestock and farm to survive. I think our security would be better served by actively learning what we face rather than leaving it to chance.

"I've been thinking about it while Jeffrey was putting the children to bed. We've already planted the vegetable garden for the spring, and summer chores haven't kicked in yet. This might be a good time to undertake an expedition. I figure we would need four people to make the trip. Any more than that and we would need to carry a lot of provisions that would only make the trip more difficult. Any fewer than that and we'd risk not having enough people to protect us all from the wild animals and other dangers we might encounter. I visited the Allegheny Plateau many times when I was a kid, and I estimate that it would take at least eight days of travel on horseback to get there, look around, and return, weather permitting and assuming we don't dally too much on the trip. That would at least give us enough time to learn what we might be facing."

I could see from Kelly's face that she was eager to react to my suggestion. "That's fine to suggest, but we only have five adults living here. We only have two horses. We also have to rely on our rapidly depleting winter food stores to keep us all fed until we can begin harvesting food from the garden in June. How can we sacrifice enough food for this trip you propose?"

"Yes, Kelly, I understand your concerns. As for our most critical resource, our food, we wouldn't need to sacrifice any more food than we'd eat during that time anyway. That concern is also a good reason to make sure we don't waste any time on the trip. We also may be able to supplement our food supplies with food we can hunt or gather along the way. The wild strawberries and huckleberries are beginning to come out at the lower elevations now, and we can harvest ramps and wild game as may be necessary. We all know how to survive in the wilderness. We certainly don't need to carry any more food than is absolutely necessary.

"As for the horses we need, I figure we'll have to use Hercules and Prince. We could also borrow one horse each from Carl's and Tim's farms down the valley. That would leave them each with at least one horse to take care of their own spring planting work while we're gone. If Carl would let us use Champ and Tim could get by without Donner, we'd have all the horses we'd need. Champ and Donner have been used for hunting trips, so they're both familiar with the steep terrain we'll have to traverse. I'd also like to ask Carl if he can spare his son, Trevor, to ride with us. He's only a year younger than Matthew and they have both spent a lot of time hunting in the mountains. I'd like to suggest that Matthew, Jeffrey, and I make up the rest of the expedition team."

"Now wait just a minute here!" Laura intervened. "I certainly don't want my son to go traipsing around in the wilderness. He's far too young for that. I also think you're too old to do all that hard riding. Besides, we depend on your knowledge and expertise to keep the farm going. You're much too valuable to us to risk you getting injured or, worse yet, killed just so you can have an adventure."

"I appreciate your concerns, Laura," I calmly reassured her. "But I'm not ready to be put out to pasture yet. We also have to remember an important point. I'm the only family member who can know what changes have occurred in those mountains because I'm the only one who had been there before the meteor. There's little value in making the trip if I'm not there to see what's changed. As long as Matthew and Trevor go with us, we'll have all the youth, muscle, and hunting skills we need to keep everyone safe. As for Jeffrey, I think he's earned an opportunity to see the wilderness for himself. He's very strong for his age, very intuitive, and has the greatest appreciation for and interest in nature of any of the younger children. I think you realize that he will want to go regardless of how you or any of us feel about it. If we tell him he can't come along, he'll be heartbroken."

Laura thought for a moment, then said, "Okay, I can accept the reasons why you need to go. But I'm still concerned about Jeffrey's safety. We don't know what's out there, but we do know there are panthers, bobcats, bears, and timber wolves all throughout those mountains. Any one of them would love to make a meaty meal of Jeffrey. The risk is just too great."

"Well, I'm not so sure, honey," Matthew replied. "Jeffrey's been hunting with me many times, and I know he understands the threats we'll face. I've trained him well on that. Also, I agree with Grandpa that Trevor and I can watch over him without making him feel overprotected. Grandpa's also correct about Jeffrey's reaction if we tell him he can't go. We both know that he'll never accept being told he can't. Do you really think you could hold him back like that? I also believe Jeffrey would be the best one to reassure the other children no matter what we find."

Laura's stern resistance began to melt away from her face as she contemplated Matthew's comments. She raised her finger to him as she began her response. "You just remember, Matthew," she scolded, "that if we let him go along, I'm holding you responsible for keeping him safe and bringing him back to me. If you don't, I can assure you that you'll never live it down."

"Well, that's all the encouragement I need," Matthew teased to lighten the atmosphere. "How do you plan to get there, Grandpa?"

"My first thought was to follow Cave Mountain Road into Smoke Hole because it's the shortest route. However, the slope on the back side of the mountain is so steep and the road has been overgrown for so long that I think it would be too hard on the horses and too dangerous to follow."

"You're right about that, Grandpa. I've used that route to go hunting on the mountain, and I have a hard time even determining where the old road goes down that side of the mountain. We'd be better off riding up the Petersburg Pike and following Smoke Hole Road into the canyon. It would be a lot easier on the horses, less work clearing the trail, and a lot quicker."

"I agree, Matthew. We can ride into Smoke Hole Canyon, turn up the North Fork Mountain trail, ride along the summit to the old Columbia Gas pipeline right-of-way, then drop down through Roy Gap to Seneca Rocks. From there, we can follow the old Mountaineer and Allegheny Highways over to Onego[1] and Harman, then turn north on the Appalachian Highway and follow it into Canaan[2] Valley and beyond. Those old roadbeds should still be in fairly good shape and the remaining bridges should get us across all the creeks and rivers. It's not the most direct route we could follow, but we'll make good time."

"If we all pull together, that'll be a good plan, Grandpa," Matthew affirmed.

"Well, with some help from the other children, I can certainly take care of the farm," Mike assured. "Now all we need is a date. The weather's been turning warm again over the past couple of days, and I think we've seen the last snow of the season. Of course, that doesn't mean much when you get up 3,200-4,400 feet on the plateau. You're going to have to be prepared for rough weather no matter when you leave this month."

"You're right, son. There's likely to be a good snow cover in places above 3,000 feet, but that will be very helpful in tracking both game and predators. I think we should plan to leave as soon as possible—maybe the day after tomorrow. That will give us all day tomorrow to plan and pack for the trip. Let's put it all to bed for tonight. I can use the extra sleep."

Having resolved the issue, we exchanged our good-nights and retired to the house. I took the lantern with me to my cabin and washed up for bed.

---

[1] Pronounced "ONE-go"
[2] Pronounced "ka-NANE"

84

# 10.  The Expedition Begins

Daylight broke late the next morning, as we awoke to a dull landscape huddled below a ceiling of low, dense, gray clouds, fog, and an occasional misty drizzle.  It was an ominous, perhaps foreboding beginning to the final day of preparation before we were to depart on the long and difficult journey to the Allegheny Plateau wilderness.  Nevertheless, the plans had been laid and the final arrangements were being made.

Jeffrey was sent to my cabin after completing his morning goat-tending jobs where I explained the plans we made for the journey and told him that he would be going.  The joy in his eyes overshadowed any fear or trepidations he may have harbored.  For him, this would be his epic transition to adulthood and the responsibilities that accompany it.  He knew the trip would be difficult and dangerous, but he faced it with the courage and eagerness of a young man tackling his first opportunity to prove himself.  Laura would struggle to make her mother's heart accept his enthusiasm, but in her mind, she knew full well that this day would have to come sooner or later.

A lively discussion accompanied a hearty breakfast.  The children were intensely curious about the big adventure, accepting it more as a thrilling experience than a fearful and frightening voyage into the unknown.  Reality probably rested somewhere in between, as all the adults realized.  It was an ambitious and unprecedented event for a close-knit family that depended so dearly on each other for its daily survival.  The stability and resiliency of that secure foundation would be tried and tested over the following days, and the significance of that reality weighed heavily in the back of everyone's mind, young and old.

When Mike's brothers, Carl and Tim, delivered their grandchildren to our house for their morning lessons, I explained the plans to them.  I showed them the body of the giant spider, and they immediately accepted the gravity of the situation.  Carl knelt down before the bucket to get a closer look at the spider.  After a few seconds of careful scrutiny, he looked up at me and said, "I know I haven't seen any large or small spiders that might resemble this one.  If they had been to our farm, I think I would have seen them in our mill, since that's where I see most of them go in the late summer months to seek shelter from the elements." Tim nodded in silent concurrence and said he'd never seen anything like it before.

Carl felt that Trevor would be eager to join us, and he agreed to lend us his horse, Donner. Tim also agreed to let us use Champ. They would return the next morning with Trevor and the horses in tow. Carl also suggested that Trevor bring his crossbow, which he often used for hunting. Although we had a Mossberg 12-gauge shotgun and a Ruger .308 caliber bolt-action rifle, Carl knew that the ammunition supply we had was critical to us, as we couldn't simply replicate it on our own. At least Carl and Trevor could replicate arrows for the crossbow in their mill, which is why Trevor had learned to use it.

Throughout the day, we built an inventory of critical supplies for the trip. Jeffrey sharpened a hatchet and machete, which we could use to clear our path and cut firewood. Laura and Kelly prepared a sack of food which included plenty of deer jerky, cured bacon strips, apples, biscuits and honey cornbread as staples to supplement whatever wild food we could harvest along the way. They also provided us with a skillet and a spatula to cook with and filled several salvaged army canteens with fresh spring water. Matthew packed some carving and boning knives we would need to dress any deer or bear carcass we could harvest and some extra horseshoes and nails in case one of the horses threw a shoe during the trip. Kelly bundled some cotton cloth strips and other first aid supplies in the event we needed them. We also packed four bed rolls, including warm clothes and ponchos to protect us from wet weather. Together with our firearms and ammunition, we would be well prepared for whatever conditions awaited us.

As the day progressed, the sullen, dreary weather that had greeted us at dawn dissipated, and we were rewarded with a bright and sunny afternoon. As evening approached, we gathered on the west-facing porch and enjoyed a glowing orange and red sunset over Cave Mountain. According to old weather lore, a red sunset portends fine and pleasant weather on the following day, which reassured us that the trip would begin on a good note.  We retired to bed early, so that all would be well-rested in the morning.

*****　*****

As we anticipated, the morning broke brisk, bright, and clear, with a delicate coat of frost on the buildings and yards.  Matthew had risen early and was in the horse barn saddling Hercules and Prince for the long journey.  It was difficult to store everything we would need, and all the saddlebags were stuffed to the gills.  Matthew strapped rifle scabbards to each horse and inserted my trusty Ruger .308 in Hercules' scabbard and the Mossberg 12-gauge in Prince's scabbard.  We decided to bring only enough ammunition as the gun magazines could handle, which was five shells for the 12-gauge and ten cartridges for the Ruger's magazine.  As long as Trevor brought a full quiver of crossbow arrows (which we knew he would), we felt we could adequately defend ourselves.

When Carl, Trevor, and his children arrived trailing Donner, Matthew strapped on a set of fully stuffed saddlebags and a bed roll.  He began chatting with Trevor as they secured and carefully tested all the straps.  I approached them when they appeared satisfied that everything was secure.

"It's good to see you, Trevor," I welcomed.  "You haven't visited us in a while.  Your mustache and beard have filled in nicely."

"Thanks, Grandpa.  I was happy to hear that you wanted me to come along.  What's all this Dad told me about a big spider?"

Matthew slapped his cousin on the shoulder.  "Follow me, Trev.  We kept it in a bucket in the barn for you to see."

With Carl in tow, we all walked to the barn where they could get a good look at it.  Matthew picked up the bucket and, without warning, promptly dumped the spider at their feet just to enjoy Trevor's startled reaction.

"Holy cow!" Trevor exclaimed as he jumped back from the carcass. "That's a real monster. I've *never* seen a spider that big before. What do you think it is, Grandpa?"

"We haven't got a clue. We found it on the ledge above the cold cellar door eating a goldfinch it had killed. All we can guess is that it might be some mutation that worked its way out from the meteor impact site up on the plateau. That's why we decided to undertake this journey. We need to see what might be happening up there after all these years."

"Do you think it's dangerous?" Trevor asked.

"I guess it could be," Matthew replied. "We watched it kill the goldfinch. It injected it several times with some sort of venom. It didn't take long for the bird to die. I'm concerned it could be poisonous to us or our livestock."

"Well, I don't blame you for being concerned," Carl said. "You all better be really careful up there. If that meteor made these spiders, there's no telling what it may have done to other wildlife up there. I'll be keeping a watch out for these things."

As Matthew scooped up the spider and tossed it in the pail, Tim arrived with his three grandchildren and Champ. The children ran straight to the house, while Tim walked over to us. Tim was never comfortable around spiders as a child, and he firmly declared his hope that he would never have to see one of them again.

Matthew and Trevor strapped the last set of saddlebags and a bed roll to Champ. Being the gentlest horse of the four that we would ride, Champ was to be Jeffrey's mount. As we finished loading down the horses, Jeffrey appeared and approached Champ, stroking his neck affectionately. He had ridden him several times before when riding around Tim's farm with his cousin, Scott.

By the time we finished securing all the gear on our horses, the entire family had gathered in the yard in anticipation of our departure. We all huddled together and prayed for a safe journey. We then exchanged hugs and kisses as we bade the family farewell. Mike assured me that he had everything under control, as he reminded me to take good care of his grandson. He warned me again that I would catch the devil from Kelly and Laura if I didn't. We then mounted our steeds and trotted down the long lane to the Petersburg Pike. Jeffrey rode beside me in the lead with Matthew and Trevor riding side-by-side behind us.

The first segment of our expedition afforded us an easy, gentle ride. Although the blacktop on the old Petersburg Pike had long since crumbled, the road bed remained in good, well-packed condition sporting only some scattered weeds and patches of grass. We made good time riding as we talked quietly amongst ourselves, enjoying the sights and sounds of a brilliant spring day. As we turned onto Smoke Hole Road, the roadbed narrowed and the rush of water in the river grew louder. I leaned toward Jeffrey and reminded him to look carefully at the low rock ledges and heavy tree branches that lined our route for wildcats. It was daylight and the risk that we would be pounced upon by a hunting panther or bobcat was very slim, but I wanted to train him to be constantly vigilant in those areas. Once we got into the deep forest wilderness, all bets were off.

Eventually, we approached Eagle Rocks, where Jeffrey and I had been fishing only two days earlier. He recognized our fishing spot and told me how much he appreciated and would remember the time we spent there talking about the great cataclysm that inevitably set into motion the long chain of events that propelled us on this expedition. As we admired the towering cliff, I told Jeffrey, Matthew, and Trevor the old legend of an early pioneer named William Eagle, who settled on the land below the cliff after having fought in the American Revolution.

As the old legend goes, Mr. Eagle kept some chickens that he couldn't protect from a bald eagle that had nested on a ledge just below the top of the cliff. The eagle would occasionally swoop down from its lofty perch and carry away his young chickens, one by one. Determined to protect them, Mr. Eagle—with some help from his neighbors—scaled the cliff and asked his friends to lower him down from the top using a heavy rope so he could kill the bird with a long hunting knife and cut down the nest. However, as he was lowered down to the ledge where the nest had been built, the adult eagle swooped down and clawed at him to protect its young. Mr. Eagle slashed wildly at the bird with his knife in an effort to defend himself, but the great bird of prey was relentless. In his desperation to slash the bird, Mr. Eagle accidentally sliced the rope that he was dangling from until only one strand remained. When he noticed how tenuous his lifeline had become, he told his friends to carefully hoist him up. Although we don't know which of the combatants was eventually victorious, we can safely conclude that when Eagle fought eagle, only one eagle won.

"Tell me the truth, Grandpa," Jeffrey said with a look of skepticism, "you made that story up, didn't you?"

"I don't know if it's true or not, Jeffrey, but that's the legend I was told to explain how the cliff was named."

I pulled on the reins and Hercules came to an abrupt stop. Jeffrey, Matthew, and Trevor pulled up beside me. I then pointed down to an old gravestone that stood adjacent to the road. "All I can tell you for certain is that this is William Eagle's grave, which proves that he was buried here. You'll just have to decide for yourself if that cliff was named for the man or the bird."

Matthew and Trevor laughed, but Jeffrey gave me a look of uncertainty. "I heard a lot of old legends about Smoke Hole Canyon, Jeffrey. My dad and Uncle Bob used to tell them to us when we gathered for Sunday dinners together. Smoke Hole is a very special place, so it's not surprising to me there would be a lot of legends about it. Whether you want to believe them or not is entirely up to you." I gave Hercules a gentle nudge with my feet, and we started off again.

As we trotted along the river, I said, "Gentlemen, to me, a peaceful ride through Smoke Hole has always been a sacred experience. When I was a young child—before the meteor—my dad would take me hunting and fishing throughout the whole canyon. I remember him telling me an old German proverb that I would think about every time I was here. 'People think a hunter is a sinner because he seldom goes to church. But, in the forest, a glance to the heavens is better than a false prayer.'

"That's the sentiment that makes me think of this canyon as a sacred place. A place where heaven, nature, and man become one. It's a little slice of Eden that makes me feel small in the face of all the imposing cliffs and mountains. It's a sense of humility that I hope each of you will feel and carry with you in your hearts. Never forget that nature is bigger and more powerful than all of us. I hope you'll appreciate and respect it with the same reverence you would hold for any other place of worship. It's a part of our natural heritage that I hope you will always remember fondly." My remarks were received with silent contemplation and consent.

For another hour or so, we rode deeper and deeper into Smoke Hole Canyon, remaining vigilant throughout for any signs of predators or the spider. We encountered nothing but birds, deer, rabbits, and squirrels. We stopped periodically to appreciate the scenery and grandeur of the canyon and to allow the horses to drink from the river and graze on the lush spring grass and wildflowers.

Eventually, we came to a fork in the road. One trail continued downstream into the canyon along the river. The other headed away from the river and began a gentle uphill climb toward the massive ridge that marked the canyon's western rim—North Fork Mountain. The shattered and crumbling remains of several buildings and broken chimneys lined the intersection marking the center of the former Smoke Hole community. The sun was high in the sky above us, and we chose to stop here for our dinner. Our afternoon ride would lead us away from the river and up to the 3,400-foot summit of North Fork Mountain, where we would leave the canyon and drop down into the North

Fork River valley. Crossing over that imposing mountain wall would be the most difficult leg of our ride on the first day of our journey.

As we continued along the North Fork Mountain trail, the road became steeper and narrower. We could no longer ride side-by-side, and we gradually shifted into a single-file procession. Soon, the trail began to wind up the mountain, and it became harder to follow. Sapling trees and bushes were beginning to grow up in our path because the trail had not been used for many years. About a third of the way up the mountain, we had to shift our positions so that Matthew could take the lead. He was carrying the machete and hatchet, which he used alternately as was necessary to cut branches and bushes out of our path.

After an hour or more of slow progress, we reached the summit of the mountain. The temperature was cooler here, and we faced a stiff breeze from the northwest. There were a lot of rock outcrops and boulders on the summit, but little vegetation. We found it easier to navigate around the scattered bushes and rocks as we turned south and rode along the ridge. It was the spectacular view that most commanded our attention. From the top of the mountain, we could see up the long North Fork River valley, where a few scattered old wildflower meadows remained. We could see the mighty summit of Spruce Knob in the distance. At 4,863 feet, Spruce Knob was the highest point in the entire 400-mile-long Allegheny Mountain range, as well as the highest point in West Virginia and the Chesapeake Bay Watershed.

The most humbling aspect of the view was the unending ripples of high mountains to our west—the direction we would be heading tomorrow. Each successive forested ridgeline seemed to pile one upon the other like rolling waves on an endless sea of forest wilderness. It was an impressively dreadful reminder that we had yet to traverse the hardest and steepest terrain of our voyage—the long arduous climb through the mountain wilderness into Canaan Valley.

We had ridden a short distance—perhaps one mile—along the summit of North Fork Mountain in quiet contemplation of the stunning view, when we approached a larger open area where a wide, sporadically overgrown path stretched before us down the western flank of the mountain and into the valley below. I immediately recognized it as the old Columbia Gas pipeline right-of-way that supplied natural gas to the now-virtually-deserted city of Harrisonburg, Virginia. I knew this path would lead us down the mountain to Roy Gap, where an old roadway would take us to Seneca Rocks, one of the state's grandest natural landmarks. That is where we would camp for the night.

Our descent down the mountain was very difficult and became more demanding as we approached Roy Gap. As with the North Fork Trail that we followed up the mountain, Matthew had to take the lead and clear out branches and shrubs that impeded our path. The density of the underbrush increased as we approached the northern rim of Roy Gap, to the point where we had to dismount and lead our horses by the reins. The uneven and rocky terrain we had to traverse made for very slow progress. When we found a moderate slope that would take us into Roy Gap, the brush became even thicker and transitioned into wild rhododendron hedges along the run that carved the gap. We slashed our way along the dense thicket for several hundred feet, before we found an opening that allowed us to cross the stream and locate the old Roy Gap roadway.

At this point, we stopped again so we could rest and allow the horses to drink from the run. Although the temperature was relatively cool, we were sweating heavily. My legs were shaky after stumbling my way down the steep mountain flank. It gave me cause to feel as though I had made a mistake in deciding to lead our expedition. However, I quickly reminded myself that I was the only one who knew the land well enough to lead it.

We surveyed our area briefly for signs of the spider or other predators. Finding none, we forged on until we saw a steep rocky ridge rise before us, topped by an imposing wall of Tuscarora Sandstone rock. I immediately recognized it as the back side of Seneca Rocks. We were finally approaching our destination for the first day of our journey.

Matthew, Trevor, and Jeffrey, who had never voyaged this far beyond the summit of North Fork Mountain, were awed by the sight of Seneca Rocks. As we passed through the narrow entrance into the North Fork River valley from Roy Gap, the view became even more imposing and dramatic. Before us stood a ten-to-fifteen-foot-thick broken wall of rock that towered resolutely 900 feet above the low hill that shouldered it. The sun, which was hanging low above the summit of Timber Ridge, cast a golden yellow glow on the rocks, adding to the drama of the scene. All thoughts of how weary we were from the tedious descent melted away under the utter majesty of the view. I instantly realized that my thoughts regarding the sacredness of Smoke Hole Canyon and our surrounding wilderness area had become tangible to them.

After spending some time appreciating the glorious view, we approached the bridge where the old Roy Gap Road crossed the North Fork River. At this point, we entered one of the grassy meadows we had seen from the summit of North Fork Mountain. Suddenly, there standing solemnly before Seneca Rocks was a largely-intact building with stone walls and a rusting metal roof. The last time I had been there was more than sixty years ago. It was the old Seneca Rocks Discovery Center, which served as an office and interpretive center for visitors to Seneca Rocks and the surrounding Monongahela National Forest.

Because I knew it was built of sturdy construction, I had anticipated that it might have survived the great cataclysm. In fact, I was surprised to see that it was in such good condition. The roof appeared to be sound, even though it had rusted extensively from years of neglect. Only a few of the large exterior windows had been cracked or broken, probably by some passing scavengers. All of the other buildings we could see that constituted the former village of Seneca Rocks were in various stages of complete dilapidation. Only the Discovery Center building remained largely intact.

We tied our horses to an old metal handrail outside the Discovery Center as we surveyed the structure. It would provide a perfect shelter for us to comfortably spend the night. The interpretive displays were largely intact, but the wording had faded over time and was only partly legible. There was scattered debris on the floors and several seats in the small theater had been ripped out, but most remained intact. We found an old stone barbecue stand in a nearby clearing and used it to cook some of our bacon. As we enjoyed a well-earned meal, I recounted the old Seneca Indian legend of Princess Snowbird, upon which the great spires of Seneca Rocks were named.

"Long before our earliest ancestors settled in this area to build our farms, all of these lands were used as sacred hunting grounds by numerous tribes of American Indians, one of which had established a small village here in the shadow of these immense rocky cliffs. This band of Seneca Indians was led for many years by a great Indian chief who had ruled the small tribe for several generations. Realizing that his life was coming to an end and having no son to succeed him, the chief urged his only child, the beautiful Princess Snowbird, to choose a husband to become the future chief of the tribe. Unable, after much careful consideration, to decide for herself which of her many suitors to marry, Snowbird devised a challenge for all of the eligible braves that sought her hand in marriage. Having deftly climbed the precipitous face of Seneca Rocks many times throughout her childhood, she vowed to marry the brave who could follow her all the way to the top of the treacherous rocks and take her hand in his. All of them tried, some of whom lost their grip on the shear rock face and fell to their deaths, but only one succeeded. He became her husband and the future chief of the tribe."

As darkness began to settle into the valley, our conversation reached a lull. Our exhaustion compelled us to sleep. We rolled out our sleeping bags and chose a spot on the worn, carpeted floor to spend the night. As I drifted off to sleep, I could hear the distant call of a wolf baying at the moon. The boundless depths of the wilderness beyond were beckoning.

# 11. Harman

When I finally woke up, I realized I had overslept. Tinted windows, low, gray morning clouds and the mighty mass of Seneca Rocks and North Fork Mountain kept the interpretive center display room (in which we had slept) dark well past sunrise. Matthew and Trevor had already risen, but Jeffrey, who was exhausted from the difficult journey and all his anticipation and excitement about it, was still asleep in a far corner of the room—away from any broken glass that might remain on the carpeted floor.

I stretched to test my muscles. As I suspected, my leg muscles were particularly sore, but the pain was tolerable. In the back of my mind, I couldn't help thinking that I would need to be more careful or my advanced age could become a debilitating liability. I often lose sight of that when work needs to be done.

I quietly walked out of our shelter through the main entrance doors, which hung somewhat loosely from a forced entry many years ago. The glass in the doors was heavily fractured, but remained intact. As I made good use of a nearby tree, I heard two of the horses softly acknowledge my presence. I walked over to them and caressed their necks, asking them quietly if they had seen where Matthew and Trevor went. They appeared quite healthy, despite the prior day's rather grueling trip. "The ride will be much easier for you today," I softly promised.

Although I knew we had to cross Allegheny Mountain today—the high summit of which marked the Eastern Continental Divide—we would be riding along the old Mountaineer and Allegheny Highway corridor, which, in the times before the meteor, was known as U.S. Route 33. This was an important and well-maintained east-west highway corridor through the high Alleghenies, which meant that we wouldn't face any dense brush clearing or difficult creek crossings. My intended destination for the day was the former village of Harman, which was roughly halfway to Elkins on the western edge of the mountains.

As I was brushing Hercules, the sound of twigs snapping behind my back startled me. I turned and saw Matthew and Trevor approaching. Trevor was carrying his crossbow, and Matthew was holding three rabbits by the hind legs that they had obviously hunted and killed. "Breakfast?" I asked.

"Of course," Matthew confirmed. "However, you might want to wait until we skin them and cook the meat first. It won't be very tasty raw."

"I doubt it'll taste much better if *you* cook it," Trevor jibed, with a smirk and a poke at Matthew's side. He then turned his attention to me. "We woke up and startled a bunch of them as we were feeding and tending the horses. Since we needed a good meal, I decided it was a good opportunity to get some practice with my crossbow. I haven't used it since hunting season last fall."

"Have the horses had anything to drink?" I asked.

"We took them over to the river for a good, long drink before we went hunting for the rabbits," Matthew confirmed. "They got all they wanted."

"Good. Jeffrey is still asleep in the building. Let's see if we can get those rabbits dressed and cooked before he wakes up." With that remark, I dug into a saddlebag to retrieve our boning and carving knives.

Jeffrey, surprised at how late he had slept, finally joined us in back of the Discovery Center as we were cooking the rabbit meat. He had heard our muted conversation and occasional laughing. We supplemented our main course of rabbit meat with some lightly toasted biscuits slathered with homemade strawberry jelly. Laura had slipped a half-pint jar of it into our saddlebag.

"How far do you figure we'll get today, Grandpa?" Matthew asked.

"At least to a community they used to call Harman. The trail should be easier to ride today, even though we have to cross over Allegheny Mountain. At least we shouldn't have to hack our way through any rhododendron

thickets.  We'll decide when we get there if we want to try to go any farther.
How far we actually get will depend upon the weather and what kind of
lodging accommodations we can find.  It's a little chilly and breezy this
morning.  It might be a colder day." I advised, as I furtively rubbed my sore
knees.

"Well, it's getting late," Trevor acknowledged, "so let's gear up and head
out."

The thin, early morning clouds had melted away, and a light ground fog
was forming as the rising sun began burning off the dew.  Once our gear was
loaded and the tension of all the straps was tested, we mounted our horses
and turned away from the now desolate Discovery Center building.  As soon as
we started riding along the old highway corridor, everyone realized that the
going would be easier.  The base of the old highway roadbed was far too
compacted for trees and dense shrubs to grow within it.  For the first time in
the prior sixteen hours or so, we were able to ride two abreast again.

We proceeded through the rubble that was once the small village of Seneca
Rocks.  Portions of the historic Harper's Store still stood, but the roof and
porch had completely collapsed from neglect and the elements.  We paused
only once on our way out of the community to allow a small group of six deer
to cross our path—four does, one fawn, and a buck.  They appeared to be
heading for an early morning drink in Seneca Creek on the north side of the
road.  They stopped and studied us momentarily when they saw us, but they
soon resumed their slow procession as they grazed their way to the creek.
Since the deer hadn't seen any humans in a long time, they displayed no
innate fear of our presence.  We sat quietly for several minutes and watched
them enjoy the cold, clear waters before resuming our journey.

We kept a steady, plodding pace until we crossed an aging concrete bridge
over Seneca Creek at the eastern edge of the Onego community.  The creek
had grown narrower and the valley progressively tighter and deeper as we
paraded farther into the rugged mountains.  The wilderness closed in around

us as we paused to survey the condition of the abandoned village. The structures here, including the ornate roadside stone wall and imposing tower of the old Bible Missionary Church, still stood proudly in the center of the village, and the condition of many of the other structures, while uninhabitable and tenuous, was better than we had seen throughout our ride—perhaps even salvageable.

Trevor dismounted from Donner to readjust his saddle straps, which encouraged Jeffrey to get down as well. Matthew and I viewed the setting from our horses. The quiet breeze and the chill of the morning air sent a quick shiver down my spine. "Looks as though people might have lingered here longer than in the other places we've passed through," Trevor casually suggested.

Suddenly, we heard the sound of a board creaking and another falling loosely into a pile of debris behind the front wall of the old church. Something sizable was roaming around in the back of the church. Matthew quickly drew his shotgun from the scabbard and dismounted from Prince, handing the reins to Jeffrey. Matthew carefully pumped the gun as quietly as he could and walked stealthily toward the church, with Trevor following closely behind. I motioned for Jeffrey to stay with the horses. They froze only momentarily when the sound of additional clattering debris broke the silence. After they crept along the standing edge of the side wall, I watched Trevor count down from three with his fingers, as they coordinated their move. In a flash, they disappeared from view behind the back of the church. A shot rang out from Matthew's shotgun, and I heard a loud growl from within the church, as the blast echoed across the narrow valley. Then Jeffrey and I saw the mass of a large black bear scramble up the hill and into the dense woods, grunting as it powered its way up the steep bank.

A few seconds later, Matthew and Trevor reappeared from the back of the church smiling at each other. "Nothing to worry about," Matthew said. "Just a lone black bear scavenging through the remains—maybe looking for a place to hide from us until we passed. I think we convinced him he was better off hiding in the woods."

"Well, I'd say we've learned two things this morning," I replied. "First, we're moving deep into the wilderness, and second, there's a very healthy volume of wildlife. Looks to me like nature has fully recovered here."

"I'll say," Trevor agreed. "But we haven't seen any evidence of those giant spiders."

Matthew, Trevor, and Jeffrey remounted their horses, and Matthew sheathed his shotgun. It was time to move on and continue our search for the spiders. At this point, the grade of the road grew steeper and the curves became tighter. Shrouded by the dense, leafy forest and roadside thickets of underbrush, our view was very limited as we climbed the challenging grade.

Higher and higher we traversed, eventually rounding a sharp, hairpin turn with the lofty summit of a high mountain (Green Knob) looming above us on the right and a steep ravine trailing below us on the left. Shortly after we turned the curve, we managed to get a splendid view of the high mountains beyond the ravine—the tops of which were dusted with glistening patches of snow. Yet the road climbed farther and steeper. Jeffrey began to feel as though we'd never stop climbing. I reminded him to watch the trees and rocky outcrops to our right carefully for predators as we proceeded. Soon, we began to notice small patches of snow in the sun-sheltered clefts along both sides of the road.

As we approached the summit of Allegheny Mountain, the forest began to thin, giving way to a high, grassy gap that was recently coated with snow. When we reached the height of the gap, the view opened completely, and we were treated to a 360-degree panorama of imposing mountain peaks. The breeze was quite bracing, but we decided to stop and let the horses rest briefly from the arduous ascent, as we enjoyed the dramatic view. I broke into our food stores and retrieved some apples which we sliced and fed to the horses as a tasty reward for their determined effort.

"We've finally reached the Eastern Continental Divide," I noted. "From this ridgeline, all rainfall ahead of us to the west of this mountain col drains into the Mississippi River system and empties into the Gulf of Mexico, while rainfall to the east drains through the Potomac River basin and into the Atlantic Ocean. We are also about two-thirds of the way across the Allegheny Mountain range, and most of the high peaks you see around you top out over 4,000 feet in elevation."

I pointed out the prominent summits of Mount Porte Crayon, High Mountain, Rich Mountain, Brierpatch Mountain, and Job[3] Knob. I also noted the roadside signs indicating the elevation of the roadway and the boundary of the Eastern Continental Divide, both of which had faded significantly with time. Matthew, Trevor, and Jeffrey were transfixed by the stunning view. Even the horses appeared to be in awe of it. Although I had seen it many times in the years before the meteor impact, this was the first time any of them had ventured this far into the high Alleghenies.

As I turned my attention from the view, I noticed that Jeffrey was staring intently at the ground just beyond the edge of the roadway. I approached with interest, and he pointed down at the snow. I immediately recognized the trail that had caught his attention—panther tracks! I waved Matthew and Trevor over to see them.

"This snow probably fell early this morning," Trevor observed. "These tracks are very fresh. The wind hasn't even had a chance to obscure them and they show no signs of melting from the sun. I'd say they were probably made sometime in the last couple of hours—at *most*. It probably crossed over the mountain to hunt for the night and is now returning home."

I agreed, as I added, "They're also heading in our direction—to the west. Let's just hope it isn't going home hungry. We'll have to be especially vigilant for the rest of our ride today." I accepted the lack of any further comments as silent concurrence. "The breeze is getting stronger. We should head down off

---

[3] Pronounced, JOBE.

the mountain so we can eat our lunch in the valley, where it will be warmer and less blustery."

With that said, we resumed our ride deeper into the mountain wilderness.

***** *****

As we descended the western flank of Allegheny Mountain, we left the light snow cover behind—and with it, our ability to conveniently track the panther. We rode on for another fifteen minutes or so, when we found a delightful little grassy glade where a mountain snowmelt rivulet emptied into Horsecamp Run. A steep, rocky bluff and the surrounding tall evergreen trees proved a good buffer from the gusty breezes.

It was about mid-day and high time for the horses to rest, drink, and eat. We decided that our breakfast had been hearty enough that we could all get by on a snack of deer jerky and honey cornbread. I knew we were now within three or so miles of Harman village—which was only, at most, a gentle twenty-minute ride away. We were making very good time—much better than I had anticipated. Perhaps, with good fortune on our side, we would be able to continue on to the Dryfork community by nightfall, which was directly below Canaan Valley.

I grabbed my trusty rifle as I dismounted from Hercules. Trevor's crossbow and Matthew's shotgun provided adequate firepower to hunt small animals or scare off a wayward black bear, but they were completely inadequate to kill an attacking panther. After tending to our horses' needs and canvasing the glade for safety, we sat together on a cluster of small boulders next to the babbling creek to enjoy our brief meal. Matthew and Trevor had engaged in a lively little conversation about their morning hunting exploits and the bear they had scared off, but Jeffrey sat quietly with an uneasy, concerned look on his face.

"What's gnawing at you, Jeffrey?" I asked, catching his attention.

"I don't know, Grandpa. I've got a funny feeling that we're being watched."

"That's a healthy feeling to have when you're this deep in the wilderness, but I wouldn't let it bother you too much. We checked this glade over very carefully before deciding to rest and eat here, and I have my rifle by my side. It's also getting late in the day for that panther to still be on the hunt. If it's smart, it's probably bedded down somewhere for the day. While we shouldn't feel too comfortable here, I think we'll be okay until we finish our lunch."

"I understand, Grandpa, but I'm not sure it's the panther that makes me feel this way. Something else just doesn't feel right."

I started scanning the tree canopy around us to relieve his concerns. While we had been watching out for giant spiders, we'd found no evidence of them. A slight breeze blew and the leaves on the low bushes began to rustle slightly. Then, in the distance, I saw Hercules lift his head, whinny softly, and stiffen alertly. Did the sound of the breeze startle him, or had something else caught his attention? I suddenly felt the hair on the back of my own neck stand on end. Jeffrey looked up at me, concerned, and asked, "Do you hear something, Grandpa?"

No sooner had he finished his question when a large brown and black panther leapt from a ledge on the rocky bluff, landing with a loud growl on Trevor's right shoulder, knocking him flat onto the ground. Matthew jumped back in shock and horror, as the panther applied its weight in an effort to pin Trevor to the ground. I instantly grabbed my rifle and quickly loaded a cartridge into the chamber.

Trevor had grabbed the panther's muzzle with both hands, as he desperately grappled with it. He alertly rolled in the direction of the panther's momentum until they were lying on their sides. I took aim, but I couldn't get a clear shot at the fierce cat. Trevor yelled in terror, and the big cat snarled and growled ferociously, as they tossed and turned on the ground, locked tightly in mortal combat. Trevor fought valiantly with his arms to block the cat's front paws, which it used frantically to slash at him.

Matthew grabbed a large, dead branch and, wielding it as a club, brought it down hard on the panther's briefly exposed head. The big cat twisted back in pain and rolled away from Trevor, having been briefly dazed by the blow. Seizing the moment, I took aim at the panther's chest and pulled the trigger. Blood spurted from the open wound, as the panther screamed in anguish and died. The entire attack had lasted only a few tense moments, but it left Trevor laying motionlessly on the ground.

Matthew leapt to Trevor's aid. The sleeve of his shirt was torn and blood was oozing from the claw marks on his shoulder where the claws of the great beast had slashed him when it pounced. Fortunately, it wasn't able to get a good grip on him when it knocked him to the ground. Matthew applied pressure to the open wound and called for a bandage. Jeffrey raced to the first aid bag and retrieved a long roll of cloth bandage. Matthew quickly wrapped the bandage around Trevor's upper right arm, and I grabbed a strong stick to use as a tourniquet. We tightened it as best we could until we felt it had constricted the flow of blood. I took a second strip and wrapped it twice again to hold the tourniquet in place and broke off the exposed ends. We then rolled Trevor on his back and tried to revive him. I slapped his face briskly.

Trevor coughed and moaned as he suddenly came to. He opened his eyes and thrashed out of reflex, as though he wasn't aware that his battle with the panther was over. "Hold on there, son," I assured in a soothing voice, "It's over. We killed it. We're tending to your wound. Are you hurt anywhere else?" I could see a red scratch on the right side of his face, but it didn't appear to be serious.

Trevor shook his head, still slightly dazed, and after taking a moment to compose himself, said in a trembling voice, "I don't think so. What happened?"

"You fell off your horse and got into a nasty argument with a panther," Matthew chided with a reassuring smile on his face to relieve the tension.

"What?" Trevor replied, still uncertain of the events.

"Son, I want you to move your hands and legs for me. Do it now." I urged.

Trevor complied, which assured us that he wasn't seriously injured. By now he was becoming fully alert. "I think I'm okay. Where's the panther?"

"Grandpa shot and killed it," Matthew replied. "But it almost looked as though you were about to get the best of it on your own. It sure scared the bejeebers out of me, but you made it a good fight. It's laying right there next to you." Matthew motioned to Trevor's right with a jerk of his head.

Trevor turned his head and saw the outstretched panther lying on its back with a river of blood pouring from the wound between its front legs. "My shoulder's sore, but I think I'm okay," he said as he shuffled his body to sit upright. We helped him to his feet and urged him to walk. After a few moments, he was walking on his own.

Jeffrey pulled on my arm. "Do you think he'll be okay, Grandpa?"

"I guess so. As long as we don't pity or coddle him too much, I think he'll survive." Matthew chuckled at my comment. I turned back toward Trevor. "You'll probably have to hold the reins in your left hand for a good while, but I think you'll be able to ride. We'll check that upper arm wound again when we bed down for the night."

"I'll be fine. It's not as painful as it looks. Thanks, Grandpa."

We took another visual survey of the glade, then packed up for the rest of our ride to Harman. I figured we could find some building that would be in good enough shape to provide us with shelter. Given Trevor's condition, it now seemed wise to go no farther than Harman, regardless of how much daylight remained when we arrived. Trevor would need the extra rest. We left the panther's body precisely where it died.

\*\*\*\*\*　\*\*\*\*\*\*

We rode slowly for another half hour when we began to see the first broken buildings of Harman, one of which had burned to the ground. As we approached the center of town, Matthew noticed a thin column of smoke rising against the imposing mass of Rich Mountain. It appeared to be on the north side of the village, directly on our route. When we reached the fork in the highway, we veered right onto the roadway that would eventually take us to Canaan Valley. We rode for another quarter of a mile before we came to a sturdy log cabin that was completely intact. The column of smoke Matthew had seen in the distance was billowing from the chimney on the far end of the cabin. Not only had we found a possible place to spend the night, but we immediately knew that someone was still living in Harman!

We dismounted at a gap in the split rail fence that lined the road in front of the cabin. A crudely painted sign nailed to one of the end posts plainly read in red letters, 'ALL SCAVINGERS WILL BE SHOT ON SIGHT.' It was an ominous message to a bunch of weary travelers. We stood at the edge of the road to study the cabin momentarily, when I heard the click of a rifle being cocked behind us.

"All right, you scavengers, don't move, and raise your hands real slow!" came a determined voice from behind.

We complied. The man moved around us to see our faces. "Okay, now state yer business!"

I looked closely at the man's grizzled face. When you see so few new people over so many years, it doesn't take too long to recognize those you've met before. I couldn't quite construct the details of his face in my mind because of his overgrown mustache and beard, but for a moment, I thought I recognized his voice. "Junior?" I asked. "Can that be you?"

The man leaned closer and squinted, as he studied me more closely. I caught a glint of recognition in his penetrating green eyes and his face relaxed. Then he lowered his rifle to his hips. "David? David Ault, is that you?"

"Yes," I eagerly replied. "What on earth are you doing here?"

"What am I *doing* here?" He repeated. "Well, by the grace of God I *live* here. Whar'd you come from anyway? Are you out huntin' this far from home?"

By now Junior realized that we posed no threat to him, and we lowered our arms. He may not be the most well-spoken person I know, but he was as outgoing, considerate, and generous as any back-woodsman can be. I estimated him to be fairly close in age to my son, Mike—perhaps 58 or so. "You might say that," I said. "I'm here with two of my grandsons, Trevor and Matthew." I pointed to each in turn. "...And this strapping, young boy on the end is my great grandson, Jeffrey."

"Is yer pa with you, Dave?"

"No, I'm sorry to say that he passed away quite a few years ago."

"Well, I guess I ain't seen either of you in a hound's age."

"I'm afraid it's been a lot longer than that, Junior. I've never owned a hound that lived for 35 years."

"Do tell!" He said as he shook his head in total disbelief. "It can't be *that* long since we last set eyes on each other. Yer making me feel old afore I've been formally introduced to these young fellas."

"Boys, this is Cletus Harman, Junior. His friends call him, Junior," I explained by way of introduction. "My dad and I met up with him about 35 years ago when we all went hunting in the North Fork River valley. His family first settled this community hundreds of years ago. Junior, I thought you'd be long gone from here by now. How's your dad doing?"

"He passed on about twenty years ago. I buried him up on that hill in the family cemetery. I live here now all by myself."

"Why are you doing that? You could have come our way and lived near us. We've got a lot of good fertile land to farm over in the North Mill Creek valley."

"Go on now, I ain't no farmer, Dave. I'm a *Mountaineer*!" He declared as he thrust his chest forward with pride. "I may scratch a little dirt so's I can plant some vegetables, but I ain't up to more farmin' than that. I hunt these woods for a livin' and go scroungin' in Elkins when I need something I cain't shoot or cut with an ax." (I knew Junior would never consider himself a scavenger—that was beneath him. Junior knew that 'scavenging' was stealing from someone and 'scrounging' was making good use of something someone else had abandoned. He understood the difference and would *never* cross that line.) "This land here has been right good to me. I don't see no need to go anywhere else."

"Are there any people still living over in Elkins?"

"Oh, they's a few who stayed behind on up the old road to Beverly, but most everyone in Elkins either died or ran off after the meteor struck. All they could do was run west or south. Folks was too afraid to go north or east. Nothin' much left for 'em that way, anyways. Not a lick of 'em could do any real hard work for themselves, and no one wanted to stay in Elkins. But they left a lot of good stuff behind, and I go over there every now and then when I need to salvage things. So, where on Earth are you headin' for way out here?"

"We're on our way to Canaan Valley. I guess I owed some of my grandkids a trip into the real wilderness." Junior just chuckled at that, revealing a few gaps in his teeth.

At this point, Junior noticed the bloody bandage on Trevor's right arm. He approached him for a closer look. "What happened to you, son?"

"Oh, I had a little run in with a panther up on Allegheny Mountain. I think I'll be fine."

"Little, you say.  Well, you don't need to be takin' any chances with an injury like that.  Don't want to see it fester none.  Why don't you folks stay here with me tonight, and we'll tend to that wound.  You cain't make it into the valley afore dark now, anyway.  Besides, y'all look like that ol' cat dragged ya 'round a while afore he got serious with ya.  Got plenty of food.  We'll have some bear stew and a mess of ramps.  How's that strike ya?"

"That sounds great, Junior.  We're much obliged."

# 12. Junior

We gave the horses a good, long drink of water from the Dry Fork River, which ran behind Junior's cabin, and bedded them down for the night. Then we washed up and joined him in his comfortably warm cabin, where he had been boiling an iron kettle of bear stew in his fireplace before he went up the hill to collect some fresh ramps. The cabin was spartanly furnished, but there was plenty of floor room for us to roll out our quilted sleeping bags for the night. Junior was a boisterous and cheerful host, and we had a lively conversation about our journey and his hunting exploits as he cooked the meal.

Eventually, I took over the chore of stirring the stew while Junior dressed Trevor's wound. No one was better skilled with local herbs and potions than Junior. In the grand scheme of things, Junior characterized Trevor's wound as 'a scratch' that would heal up just fine in a few weeks. He applied a salve that he knew would prevent any infection and speed his recovery. Trevor felt no worse for the wear, and he experienced only a slight twinge using his arm.

As we sat down to eat supper around Junior's hand-made table, he began to press for more details about why we were venturing so far into the wilderness. He'd canvassed the woods so thoroughly that he knew we hadn't been out his way since I first met him so long ago. I decided it was time to tell him about the spider. I told him how Paul had discovered it down at our cold cellar, and I described it to him in detail.

"Well, I can tell ya I ain't seen no spider like that 'round here. I've hunted 'round these woods for all my life, and I ain't seen the likes of it. What makes you think you'll find some in Canaan Valley?"

"I don't know, Junior. We've been thinking it might be something that mutated after the meteor struck. My Uncle Bob, who was a doctor, believed that the bugs from the meteor debris would affect a lot of other organisms in ways he couldn't predict. That spider is the first thing we've found since then that makes us think he might have been right."

"Well, that's a real hum-dinger, I do declare. So, you think you'll find more of 'em up in Canaan Valley, eh?"

"Either there or higher up on the plateau where the debris from the meteor landed."

"Y'all don't need to look for 'em up on the plateau. That place is nothin' but a wasteland. That meteor blowed down the whole forest, and all the wildfires it caused burned the soil down to bare rocks in most places. They's no good humus left fer anything to grow in. I've checked up there from time to time to see if anything was goin' to grow back, but all I ever found is some patches of scrub brush and grass. It'll be a long time afore they's enough soil built up to support any trees. Nothin' left but scrub and rock, I tell you.

"Now, Canaan Valley did eventually recover, but what trees you'll find up there still ain't very big. It takes a long time fer tall trees to grow in that miser'bly cold valley. I can find a good supply of deer and a few bears that feed on the huckleberries and cranberries that grow up there, but the *real* feast is along the slopes of the Allegheny Front and in my valley. Y'all are welcome to go see for yourself, but don't expect too much. It's not at all what you might remember from the time afore the meteor."

Junior's explanation started to make me think we made a mistake in planning this trip. Perhaps the spider we saw was something new and unique. It was almost impossible for me to believe there couldn't be a lot more of them out there *somewhere*—but where should we look for them? Junior took a few more spoonfuls of stew, and then looked up and raised his eyebrows as though something had just occurred to him. He rubbed his chin pensively, as he looked directly at me.

"You know, Dave, I know I ain't seen this spider of yours, but I have seen somethin' strange that I cain't explain. I go huntin' all 'round these parts at least once a week. Over the past few years, I have seen a bunch of rabbits, raccoons, and even a few baby deer just lyin' dead in the woods. It's mighty strange."

"That doesn't seem all that strange to me, Junior. There's plenty of wolves, panthers, bobcats and other predators out there looking for food. Why do you find it strange that you'd stumble across their prey?"

"Yer forgettin' somethin', Dave. All the predators out there are huntin' them animals for food. If they kill it, they's gonna eat it, right? Well, I've been findin' dead animals that are intact. I don't see so much as a bite or a scratch on them. I realize that some young wolves or panthers might play with rabbits and things so's they can learn how to hunt. I also know some animals just up and die. But I keep findin' more and more animals that don't look like they've been touched. How do you explain that? You told me this big spider of yours may be poisonous, and that it sucks fluid from its prey. Do you reckon they might be killin' these animals I keep findin'?"

Everyone at the table looked directly at me. "I don't know, Junior, but that's a great question. Maybe we do need to take a closer look up there, after all."

"If you don't mind, I think I'll go along with ya, Dave. You could use a person with some good trackin' skills, and I'd sure like to know for myself."

No one objected. We soon finished our meal and cleaned up all the supper remains. We then bedded ourselves down for the night. Tomorrow promised to be an interesting day.

***** *****

I had a restless sleep that night. I heard sounds outside the cabin that made me realize something had startled the horses. I got up as quietly as I could (so I wouldn't disturb the boys) and went to the door to check on them. I stood momentarily on the large, flat rock that served as the cabin's front door stoop to survey the surroundings. The sky was clearing and the moon was nearly full, casting black shadows around the yard. There was a large silky halo around the moon which suggested to me that some rain would fall the next day. On the far side of the yard, I could see the dark outlines of the horses, which we had tied to trees lining the creek, as they pawed and fidgeted nervously in response to some unseen threat.

I saw nothing out in the open yard, so I decided to venture toward the horses, carefully scanning the shrub- and tree-line for any signs of a potential predator. There was no breeze, but I heard the soft rustle of leaves from one of the nearby bushes, as I crossed the yard. I froze at the sound and turned slowly in its direction, trying carefully not to startle and scare away whatever might be there before I had a good chance to see it. At first, I didn't see anything, but then another nearby shrub jiggled slightly. As I focused my eyes on it, I noticed a steady, unblinking glare from what appeared to be two sets of four yellow-green eyes glowing back at me through the leaves, roughly two feet above the ground. Perhaps I was seeing a pair of hunting animals. Whatever it was struck me as being about the height or size of a wildcat (which would more likely be a solitary hunter) or a wolf (which *does* hunt in packs), but the strange alignment of the eyes that glowed back at me just didn't make immediate sense to me. I wasn't at all sure of what I was seeing.

I felt the creature's intense stare penetrate into the depths of my mind. I stood there, motionless, not quite certain of which one of us was studying the other. We seemed to be caught in mutual evaluation of each other, perhaps driven as much by scrutiny as by fear. Another chill ran down my spine, as I contemplated its motives and my next move. I couldn't see the body of the animal staring at me, but I could sense an unsettling intellect behind its piercing, intense glare. This was *not* the ravenous glare of some typical predator caught unexpectedly, as it stalked its prey. It felt more like it was studying me carefully to decide whether or not I posed a threat to it.

I heard the leaves rustle slightly again, but the eyes remained still and focused. There was *definitely* something or a pair of relatively large animals there. Were they digging in for a sudden attack? No, they just continued to stare at me. Our stalemate wore on my mind. It seemed to me like time had stopped. One of us had to make a move, or we might end up spending the rest of the night just staring at each other. I swallowed my initial fear and indecision and began to approach slowly, confirming to it that I knew something was there. I saw no reaction to my first short, tenuous steps, so I casually stopped again to demonstrate that I was not trying to threaten them. It seemed they understood. The leaves jostled again only slightly as one or both of them adjusted its position. Still, the glowing green eyes stared back at me. Why didn't I see them blink? How long could they hold a stare without blinking? ...And why did they appear to have *four* eyes? I wished Junior was standing here with me. He would probably know what it was from experience.

I was now about eighteen feet from the shrub line where they were hiding. I decided to take a few more innocent and nonthreatening steps toward it. I took three more steps before I heard the leaves rustle again and stopped. This time, both sets of eyes shifted simultaneously to the right—away from the center of the bush—but whatever they were, the creatures continued to hold their ground. However, the fact that both sets of eyes shifted simultaneously suddenly made me realize that the glowing eyes belonged to one creature not two. But how could that be? I knew of no large creature that would have *two* sets of four eyes, much less one.

Many questions swirled in my mind. What was it? Was it preparing to pounce on me? Was it simply trying to get a better view? Was it making its last stand to intimidate me before retreating? Again, I sensed the creature's intellect as it tried to interpret my actions and decide what to do in response.

I felt like we were locked in a strategic game of move and countermove. It was not simply reacting to me, or it would have attacked me or retreated at my first approach. We were actively studying and contemplating each other. Did I dare to pursue it further? I was so focused on the mind game we appeared to be playing that I hadn't seriously considered what consequences I might face. I decided to take a step back to see if I could draw it out from the bush. However, as I began to move, I saw the eyes abruptly disappear, and I heard the creature suddenly retreat, its body and feet moving quickly, pattering in the dried leaf litter that covered the ground as it scrambled away through the underbrush. I rushed forward, not in pursuit, but in an effort to catch a glimpse of it before it escaped.  By the time I reached the bush, it had been swallowed up by the dark shadows of the woods.

A few moments after it left, the horses settled down.  I gave them a reassuring pat on their necks to help calm them.  I knew the encounter was over, but I felt I had learned nothing meaningful from it.  I simply couldn't decide what it was, and I was very disappointed that it had escaped before I could catch a clear glimpse of it.  As I crept quietly into the house and went back to bed, my mind scanned through images of all the different wild animals I knew to be in its presumed size range.  I simply couldn't reconcile the eyes.

I didn't get much sleep after the encounter.  Every time I dozed off, I would see the glowing, yellow-green eyes in my dream, and they would wake me up.  After two or three failed dreams, it hit me.  Most of the spiders I've studied have two sets of four eyes.  But how could that be?  The creature would have to have been much larger than the big spider we found.  Could they possibly get any bigger than the one we had seen?  No, that just didn't seem reasonable.  Still, I couldn't put the nagging thought out of my mind.

# 13. Canaan Valley

Junior made sure we all got an early start to the day. It was his habit, being the skilled and experienced hunter that he is. Besides, an early start was essential if we wanted to have enough daylight to conduct a fairly thorough survey of the valley. I decided not to mention my nighttime encounter with the creature until I had more information to understand it better. Given the sarcastic sense of humor of my traveling companions, it would have been the butt of jokes, anyway. I just busied myself with my final preparations for our trip.

Jeffrey caught me by surprise. "What are you writing, Grandpa?"

"Oh, I'm just making a few notes for myself." I nervously replied, as I quickly closed the book.

"I've seen you writing in that black book quite a few times over the past few days. What is it?"

"This?" I held up the six-by-nine-inch dark brown, leather-bound book I had been carrying with me since I first told Jeffrey the story of the meteor. It was an old, largely blank diary I had removed from my wife's shoe box of mementoes earlier that day. I wasn't sure how I wanted to explain it to him. "Well, Jeffrey, when you get to be my age, it gets hard to remember things. I just wanted to scribble down some notes about our trip so I could remember them. That's all."

"But I saw you writing in it on your porch the day I came to you with the fossil."

"Yes, well, to tell you the truth, I don't know the best way to explain it to you now. I'll tell you more about it later—when the time is right. For now, we've got to get ready for our ride."

"Okay, Grandpa. I'm ready."

As we finished strapping our bed rolls to the horses, Junior presented me with an item he insisted we should add to our gear. It was something I had not seen in more than forty years—a hand-held flashlight, complete with working batteries! None of the boys had seen one before, and they were impressed by the bright beam of light it produced. Junior had 'salvaged' a bunch of them from an old abandoned store in Elkins and decided to make a gift of one to us. "I cain't say how long those batt'ries will work. They's pretty old and, if they work at all, they sure don't last long, but y'all should get some good use out of it afore they die," Junior advised. I thanked him for the useful gift. Junior also loaded and packed his .30-06 Winchester rifle.

A dry weather front apparently swept across our area the previous day and carried with it a warmer, more humid air mass with numerous billowing cumulus clouds. The breeze had shifted from the west wind that we faced yesterday to a somewhat stronger southwest flow by morning. The sun was bright and intense and quickly burned off the morning chill, as we headed north from Junior's cabin. Junior was riding the larger of his two mules—the one he called Bruno. A mule is a very practical beast of burden for a hunter, as it can comfortably traverse the roughest terrain, and it is far less skittish than the average horse, which is why it is often used as a protective companion animal for small livestock, such as goats and sheep.

We were now following the old Appalachian Highway that was once designated on road maps as West Virginia Highway 32. The roadway climbed gently as we rode upstream against the flow of the accompanying river. At this point in our journey, I deliberately slowed our pace so we could more closely survey the roadsides for signs of our quarry. However, I was very careful to avoid explaining why or what I had seen last night. It didn't matter, anyway. We failed to see any of the giant spiders.

About an hour later, we had reached the former community of Dryfork. This was the point at which the roadway left the river behind and began the long, steep ascent into Canaan Valley. Junior recommended that we stop briefly to allow the horses to get a good drink before the long climb. It would be more than an hour's grueling uphill ride before we could reach the next convenient watering spot.

Junior, who had taken the lead, directed us to an old country store that was partially overgrown with a dense mat of long, scraggly honeysuckle vines. We dismounted and stretched our legs, while Matthew and Trevor led the animals across the road to the river. Junior, always the opportunist, used the time to sort through some of the building debris to look for any potentially useful item he might have overlooked before. He was inside the crumbling building, when I heard him surreptitiously call my name, as he urgently waved for me to join him.

I entered the dilapidated structure. Junior motioned me to approach him quietly. "I think we're bein' watched," Junior whispered in my ear. "It's over there at the edge of the woods." Junior was pointing at a hole in the back wall to the woods on the hill behind the store. "I heard some movement in the brush."

"Did you get a look at it?" I whispered back to him.

"I seen the body of some animal, but I couldn't make out what it was. I reckon it was about two feet long and about eighteen inches high. It looked to be black, which is why I could make it out in the shade of the shrubs. It was too small to be a panther or a wolf, and it's gettin' a little late for them to be out and about, anyway. Might have been a bobcat, or a bear cub, but they wouldn't be watching us. This thing didn't just run off when I started roustin' about in here."

My mind immediately turned to the creature I had encountered the previous night. "Are you sure it's gone?"

"Yeah, I seen the bushes rustle as it fled up the hill. Too late to chase after it now. By the time we could get all the way 'round the building, it'd be halfway up the hill."

"Let's see if we can find some tracks."

Junior and I left the building through a gap in the front wall and went around the back to the spot where the creature had been. The ground was matted with dried leaves and evergreen needles, making it unlikely the creature would leave any discernable tracks. As we came back around the building, Matthew and Jeffrey were waving excitedly for us in front of a partially collapsed building directly across the road.

"Come see what I found in here," Jeffrey urged. He led us through the door and pointed to what appeared to be a translucent white carcass in the corner of the room.

Junior picked it up by a couple of opposing long tendrils and held it out to me for closer inspection. It was the confirmation I had half-expected when I first saw it from the doorway. "I know what that is, boys. It's the molted remains of a spider's outer skin. See, it has eight legs and an articulated body—here's the thorax and here's the abdomen," I said pointing to the appropriate body parts. "Spiders shed their skins as they grow."

"Must be the spider you told me about," Junior offered. "Look at the size of it."

"Yeah, that's what concerns me. This skin is at least twice the size of the spider we found. That means the one we found wasn't fully mature. These things can grow to be a lot bigger than we thought."

It was then that I decided to mention the encounter I had at Junior's place. The story didn't sound so crazy anymore.

"You mean to tell me these things have been watchin' me without my knowin' it? You'd think I'd have found one of these skins afore now."

"Maybe not, Junior. When spiders shed their outer skin, they are very vulnerable. They can't even move fast to escape a predator. That's why they look for a very secluded spot to hide in while they molt. You wouldn't find one somewhere out in the open. When you consider how many spiders you see, it's very rare to find one of their molted skins. This one is just so big that it was easy to find in the corner of the building. There's so many old, abandoned buildings around these parts that they provide a convenient hiding place to molt. We just didn't think to look closely in all the old buildings we passed by for evidence of them."

"I still cain't figure why I ain't seen one out in the woods."

"When you're hunting, you're tracking game. You're looking for certain tracks, not just any old tracks. The feet of these spiders are so small, they might not leave any identifiable tracks in the woods. Perhaps they can climb the trees or hide in the bushes when they see you coming. They may be big for spiders, but it isn't hard to believe they'd be difficult to see when you don't know to look for them."

"Ya may be right, Dave."

"What should we do now?" Matthew asked.

"Well, I think we should at least see if we can find any more evidence of them as we go into the valley—now that we know more about what we're looking for," I said. "Perhaps there'll be more of them up there, so they'll be easier to find. At least if we don't actually see one, we've learned that they get a lot bigger than we thought. The amount of venom a spider as big as the one that left this molted carcass behind could produce might be pretty dangerous. If we're likely to encounter more of them in the future, it pays for us to know what we're up against. We just need to be more vigilant of them as we go along."

With that said, we retrieved our horses and resumed our ride up to the high valley with renewed determination. The grade of the road became steeper and steeper as we rode along. Eventually, the hills on either side of the road closed in on us. We passed through a steep, rocky gap, and the grade of the road became steeper again.  The roadway began to twist slightly, until we saw a second rocky gap before us.  As we approached it, I spotted a cave in the outcropping ledge.

"Junior, is that a cave on that ledge?"  I asked pointing to it.  "I've been up this way before, and I don't remember seeing one."

"Oh yeah," he replied.  "That cave didn't appear until after the meteor. The explosion made the ground shake so hard that some of the ledge fell and the cave opened up.  No one knew it was there afore."

Thinking back more carefully, I realized that I hadn't been up this far since the meteor fell.  As we passed through the second rocky gap, we encountered a pile of boulders and rubble that had collected at the base of the ledge and covered two-thirds of the roadway, forcing us to pass through single file.  I estimated we were now within twenty or so miles of 'ground zero,' and it surprised me that I hadn't noticed any other land- or rock-slides until now.

We had watched carefully for evidence of giant spiders as we passed through both rocky gaps.  Again, we saw nothing.  If the one I thought I saw in Junior's back yard had followed us to Dryfork, it had given up before we reached the rocky gaps.  There was no place for it to hide from view in the exposed gaps.

We rode for another fifteen or more minutes after passing through the second gap, and we found ourselves at the south rim of Canaan Valley.  The Blackwater River, which drains the valley, flows north-by-east for a good distance before twisting back to the west, which meant that we had a spectacular view of the valley when we reached the rim.  Matthew, Trevor, and Jeffrey were clearly impressed by the sweeping vista, so we stopped and dismounted to appreciate it.  At this point, I decided to assume the role of a tour guide for our first-time visitors.

"We are now at a gap in the southern rim of Canaan Valley.  The floor of this valley rests at 3,200 feet or so above sea level, which makes it one of—if not *the*—highest mountain valleys in the eastern part of our country. The mountain that forms the eastern edge of the valley is Cabin Mountain, which attains a summit elevation of nearly 4,500 feet. The ridge on the western edge is Canaan Mountain, which tops out at just over 4,000 feet. Beyond this valley to the north and east is Dobbin Ridge and the vast Allegheny Plateau, where the meteor fell some sixty years ago. Since we already know the plateau remains a wasteland, we won't be continuing on to it. Junior's been there recently, and he saw no evidence of the spiders over there. Perhaps all animal life on the plateau was wiped out, and there's not enough soil or forest to support any significant amount of wildlife yet.

"In the times before the meteor struck, there were two large ski resorts along the west face of Cabin Mountain—Canaan Valley and Timberline. They built many homes at the ski areas and along the main highway that runs the length of the valley. I remember seeing quite a few restaurants and tourist businesses along the highway, too. They were all designed to make a lot of money from tourists, so they were built as inexpensively as possible. The meteor explosion and subsequent wildfires would have wiped them all out."

Plant life in the valley, from our vantage point, was varied. Most of the land was covered with a meadow that I knew would be swampy because the Blackwater River and its tributary streams had large floodplains. We saw numerous groves of short trees (relative to what I remembered prior to the meteor), but they clearly indicated that the valley was in active recovery. The taller tree stands marked the areas I suspected to be farthest from the flooding influence of the Blackwater River. The transitional areas between forest and swamp were covered with low bushes and scrub-brush, which represented the best source of food for recovering wildlife in the valley. Looking closely along the nearby edges of the swamp, I could see the scattered, charred and stubby remains of many older big trees that were knocked down and burned by the blast.

As I glanced to the left, just below the eastern face of Canaan Mountain, I noticed the shattered remains of a multi-story building that was once the main resort hotel for the former Canaan Valley State Park. The roof, all of the fourth floor, and a good part of the third floor had been ripped off the building. Soot and scorch marks from subsequent wildfires marred the remaining portions of the structure. The lower floors of the building didn't look very sound, but enough of it stood to provide a potential home or hiding place for the giant spiders. I decided we should take a closer look at it. If we were going to find any evidence of the spiders in this valley, I figured we'd find it there, first. Junior agreed.

We trotted slowly down the south rim and headed toward the old resort hotel. Along the way, we found a small pool of fresh water to give our steeds a chance to drink. While they were drinking, Junior walked around the surrounding scrub as though he was searching for animal tracks. After roaming aimlessly for about fifteen minutes, he waved me over to a spot he had found. I walked to him with Matthew, Trevor, and Jeffrey following closely behind. When we joined him, we learned that Junior wasn't looking for animal tracks after all.

"Looky here," he directed. "See this little pool of water in the rocks?"

We all gathered down and studied it. The water had an orange tint to it, and it was covered by a layer of scum with a network of thin white roots weaving a floating mat across it. It was now Junior's turn to play tour guide.

"My pa showed me this orange scum a long time ago. He was one of the local people all the scientists hired to lead them to the meteor site after it struck. He said they found lots of this scum up on the plateau. He'd never seen the likes of it afore. People wasn't sure if the government scientists put it there to scare us off or the meteor caused it, but everyone figured it caused all the sickness. Back then, you could only find it on the plateau. About the time that Pa died, we started findin' it down here in the valley. You reckon it's what made the giant spiders, Dave?"

"If my Uncle Bob was still here, he might think so. He was one of the first people to study it after the meteor fell. He said that it contained traces of organic matter from some other world outside our solar system. That organic matter from the meteor probably caused both the orange scum and the disease that killed everyone later on. I don't think the orange scum is deadly, in and of itself; it's just evidence of how alien microbes in the meteor can cause earthly life to mutate. It caused many simple organisms, like the virus that killed everyone, to mutate and become deadly. Think of it this way, an empty gun laying on the ground isn't deadly. However, if you pick it up, load it with ammunition, point it at someone, and pull the trigger, it becomes deadly. The alien microbe that landed with the meteor was just the bullet that nature needed to teach us a humbling lesson.

"Uncle Bob realized that the alien microbe caused the simple organisms, like algae and other viruses to mutate, but he also believed that it could eventually affect more complex animals over time in ways we couldn't imagine. I'm sure he'd think the spiders we are finding are evidence that's occurring in our time. He'd want to analyze them to be sure, especially because it's happening so soon after the meteor struck. Unfortunately, we don't have the ability to analyze it as he would, so we may never know for certain. All I can say is that I think we've moved deep into the spiders' home territory, and they're just starting to spread out to our areas.

"Uncle Bob believed that the natural world was more powerful and complex than we think. He used to say that whenever one life form disrupted the delicate balance of nature too severely, nature would find a way to fight back and restore that balance. He said that the virus the meteor delivered to Earth was just nature's way of keeping our human population in balance. Maybe the spider is nature's way of taking the fight to the next level. I don't know how we can be sure of what's going to happen over the next 100 years or more. I only know that we don't have all the answers, and we don't have the power to reverse whatever course nature will take."

The look I saw in Jeffrey's eyes told me that he understood what I was implying. Like me, he suspected that the spiders' copper-based blood, which could have resulted from a much earlier meteor impact from the same original planet in a distant solar system, may explain why the spiders had mutated so quickly. What might a second, reinforcing infusion of viable alien genetic material have done to them as they reproduced generation after generation over the past 60 years? I could almost see his mind working on that critical question, as I studied the brooding look on his face. However, he said nothing, because he knew it was a question I couldn't answer, and that Junior and the rest of our party wouldn't understand at this time. At that moment, I knew Jeffrey was the only member of our party who had the combination of curiosity, common sense, and cool, keen intellect to put all the pieces together so quickly in his mind.

"Well, I ain't about to let a bunch of spiders chase me off my huntin' grounds!" Junior adamantly proclaimed.

"If they've been here as long as they appear to have been and you haven't seen them before now, I'd wonder how much of an immediate threat they really are. If I did see one of them in your backyard last night, it seems to me that they could have killed all of us right then and there, but they didn't. Who knows how long they've been watching you?"

Junior shrugged his shoulders, perhaps because he didn't have an answer to my question or because the thought of it sent a chill down his spine—or both. He just turned away, lost in his own thoughts, and headed back to the horses. We all followed silently behind him.

We continued on to the old resort hotel building. Using the flashlight that Junior gave us and one of his own that he brought along, we carefully walked around the first floor of the building. Sixty years of harsh Canaan Valley weather had taken its toll on the remnants, and repeated rains, freezes, and thaws caused the first-floor ceiling to collapse in many places. Not only was the building a poor shelter from the elements, we became concerned that it might not stand up to a good stiff wind or a heavy snowfall. The building was empty and dangerous. It creaked with every stiff breeze. After carefully completing our cursory survey of the structure and finding no evidence of spiders, we decided to enjoy our noon-time meal outside in the warmth of the sun.

Junior entertained us during our meal with stories of his many hunting adventures in Canaan Valley. All the while, the intensity of the heat and humidity continued to build. The few tall, puffy clouds we saw forming in the morning became bigger and more numerous as the day progressed. By early afternoon, some of them began to assume an anvil shape with large, trailing tops and dark gray bases. It became obvious that we were facing a good chance of severe afternoon thunderstorms, and we were too far from Junior's house to make it all the way back before they unleashed their fury on us. We desperately needed to find some shelter.

None of the buildings we had passed on our ride were adequate to protect us from the severe storms that were brewing. Most of them had only partial roofs or none at all, and those that did offer some cover from the weather were of questionable stability. Trevor noted the cave we had passed in the last rocky gap before we reached the valley rim. It was our only choice, but we knew we'd have to check it thoroughly for the giant spiders before deciding to wait out the storm there. Having no other reasonable choices, we mounted our steeds and started back the way we had come. All the while we were riding to the cave, the south wind was building and the sky to the south and west was becoming very dark and foreboding.

The cave opening stood nearly thirty feet above the roadway and could only be accessed by climbing the rocky rubble pile that lay beneath it. Our first concern was what we were going to do with the horses. There was no obvious way to contain or corral them. They couldn't climb the steep rubble pile, and there were no rock ledges that they could stand beneath for shelter. We finally decided that we would have to lead them down below the rock gap and tie them to trees that afforded them the best protection and were least likely to topple if the winds became strong. The wind was already threatening to do so when we arrived there. Matthew and Trevor decided they would tie down the horses.

That meant that Junior, Jeffrey and I would have to scale the rock pile and survey the cave. Matthew handed me the shotgun. Junior decided he didn't need his rifle, because we felt the shotgun would be adequate protection against any spider we might find. Jeffrey and Junior carried the flashlights. Since Jeffrey could scramble up the rocks faster than we could, he took the lead and I followed, as we assaulted the giant rubble pile. Thunder was already rumbling in the distance when we finally reached the entrance to the cave. The entranceway was about ten feet high and wide, and the passageway beyond appeared to maintain those dimensions for a distance, within a reasonable degree of flexibility to account for randomly protruding rocks.

I took the flashlight from Junior's hand and handed him my shotgun. In the dark, shadowy environment of the cave, I figured he would be a better shot than me. It was too dark in the cave to know how deep it was. We turned on our flashlights and shined them into the depths of the opening. It was immediately clear that the passage bent off to the right about sixty feet into the cave, but we couldn't see beyond that point. I suggested I would lead with Junior following behind me with the shotgun. Jeffrey would follow behind and do his best to shine his flashlight around us.

We took our first few tenuous steps into the cave very cautiously and slowly, reacting occasionally to the sudden rumbles of thunder behind us. The roof was about four feet above our heads and had no apparent shafts that a spider could hide in to drop down on us from above. The floor was uneven and littered with gravel and debris that crunched under our feet with every step we took. If there was a spider hiding around the bend, our flashlight beams and the crunching sounds we made as we advanced gave it adequate forewarning that we were approaching.

When we reached the bend in the cave, Junior stepped up by my side. I edged along the left wall of the cavern, so I could gradually shine the flashlight into the curve. The bend was fairly sharp, but I was able to see clearly into it. I took one quick step into the curve, and was relieved to find that the shaft extended fairly straight for another 150 feet or more from my position, and I was able to see deep into the cave. I scanned the ceiling and each wall carefully. I saw nothing there. We decided there was little need to go any farther. The cave appeared to be safe enough for us to shelter briefly there during the storm.

By the time we returned to the entrance, we could hear Trevor and Matthew calling for us from below. We told them the cave was safe and waved for them to climb up and join us. As they scrambled over the final few rocks, the sky opened up and the anticipated deluge descended upon us. A relentlessly strong wind whistled and howled through the rock gap outside the cave entrance, and we huddled about twenty feet from the opening to wait out the storm.

# 14. The Cave

Lightning flashed so frequently that the thunder could barely keep up with it. The thunder gradually became more of a constant rumble broken by occasional loud claps as it echoed through the gap and down the length of the cave. The noise was so loud that we couldn't even talk to each other while the storm raged. We had the shared impression that the world was coming to an end. We kept the flashlights on throughout the storm so we could maintain our vigilance for giant spiders, although we saw none.

After fifteen or twenty minutes of intense rain, gusty winds, lightning, and thunder, the storm began to subside. Trevor was the first to speak.

"We had a hard time finding a good sheltered stand of trees to tie down the animals. They were so frightened by the sound of the approaching storm that they struggled against us. I'm concerned that one or more of them may have broken free. We may have to search for some or all of them after the storm has passed."

"I'm afraid my knees are pretty sore from all the riding and walking we've done over the past few days," I replied. "I had a hard time climbing up here to the cave. How far away did you go to tie down the horses?"

"We found a little grove of trees about 150 feet from the base of the rubble pile," Matthew said. "There's some steep and rocky terrain just beyond the rocky gap that you have to negotiate just to get to the horses. Maybe you'd better just wait up here until we can bring them back."

"That's fine, but Junior and Jeffrey will have to go with you in case you need to search for the horses. Our horses aren't familiar with this territory, so they may not be able to find their way back on their own. You may need all the manpower we can muster."

"Are you sure you'll be safe?" Trevor asked. "We could be gone for a spell."

"As long as I've got the shotgun and the flashlights, I should be fine right here. We checked deep into the cave and it looked clear for more than 200 feet beyond the entrance. I'll just sit here by the entrance and rest. By the time you come back with the horses, I should be rested enough to ride comfortably."

The rain had finally stopped, but the thunder could still be heard faintly in the distance. Matthew walked to the entrance and looked up at the sky. "The clouds are breaking and the sun should come out soon. I think we'd better go after the horses right away. The sooner we get to them, the better the chance that we won't have to look far to find them."

Everyone agreed, and one by one, the boys began their climb down the rubble pile. I moved over to the entrance and leaned the shotgun against the wall by my side. I watched as Jeffrey scrambled down the rocks, and they disappeared from view around the edge of the gap. A few moments later, the afternoon sun broke through the clouds and shined into the cave on me. I sat for at least fifteen minutes appreciating the fresh scent of the air and the sounds of the birds chattering around the cave entrance. The storm had washed all the humidity from the air, and the temperature dropped at least fifteen degrees. A cricket began to chirp somewhere down the shaft from me, and his lilting call combined with the comfortable warmth of the sunlight made me drowsy. I was far more tired than I had realized. Shortly thereafter, I nodded off to sleep.

***** *****

I can recall having a very peaceful dream. The first in many nights. I was home on our farm, surrounded by my family. We were sitting on the farmhouse porch at dusk, watching the youngest children chase fireflies in the yard while the crickets chirped, and we adults were laughing quietly and talking amongst ourselves in the soft, muted voices that always feel appropriate for that setting. Then, I felt the presence of Jeffrey, seated on the porch beside my chair, tugging gently on my arm.

Suddenly, I felt a sharp, stabbing pain on the ankle of my left leg! I yelled in agony and writhed back and forth on the ground. As my body twisted, I felt my left arm bump into something, as it fell away from me. My ankle felt as though it was on fire. The pain was excruciating, and I couldn't contain it. For a few moments, I thought my foot had been cut off. I began to gain consciousness, as I grabbed my left ankle and pulled myself up into sitting position. I was still grimacing from the shooting pain.

When I managed to open my eyes, I immediately realized I had rolled to the opposite side of the cave entrance. I turned to my right and there, in the retreating darkness of the cave stood a giant black and red-spotted spider. I instinctively froze at the sight of it and swallowed my agony as best I could. Quickly scanning the opposite wall of the cave, where I had originally sat down to rest, I noticed the shotgun lying flat on the cavern floor against the wall. I had knocked it over when the spider injected its venom into my ankle. The fire I felt from its bite throbbed in my ankle far more painfully than any charley horse cramp I had ever experienced.

I shook my head to clear my mind, perhaps to shake off my disbelief at the sight of the spider. It was huge! It appeared to be more than twice the size of the one we first saw over the door to the cold cellar. Its body was at least two feet long, and its legs were of equal length. From my seated position on the floor, it stood as tall off the floor as my shoulder. As I drank in the sight, I realized that it was just standing there before me. Was it studying me, stunned by my reaction to its bite, or simply waiting patiently for me to die? I couldn't be sure, but I felt that it was acting inquisitively just as had the creature that spied on me the night before—AND as *I* had studied the original spider we found at the cold cellar!

I realized, at that very moment, why I felt the spiders were intelligent. It was because I was seeing them acting the *same way* I did when I studied the first spider we discovered. They didn't seem to be acting or reacting out of blind instinct. Their behavior was cool and collected. They seemed to be in control of their reactions and deliberately inquisitive in their conduct. Just as the monster that stood only two feet from my leg was acting now. It just stood there as though it was either stupefied or quietly calculating its next move. My mind chose the latter. It could have stabbed me again at any moment during my drowsy struggle to finish me off, but it didn't. It just held its ground like a sentinel, neither fleeing in fright nor attacking out of malice or hunger. Perhaps it was surprised by my violent reaction to the sting.

We simply stared at each other quietly for several minutes, as I massaged my aching ankle. I could feel a large welt forming where it had bit me. My left foot was becoming numb. I felt vulnerable under its intense gaze. Was it trying to lull me into submission or hypnotize me with its cold, steady stare? In my foggy, painful state, I couldn't take any chances. I slowly slid my right hand to my side to withdraw the hunting knife I had strapped to my belt. When I felt that I had a firm grip on the handle, I swiftly drew the knife from its sheath, brandished the gleaming blade before the spider, and leaned toward it to convey that I meant business.

The spider reacted immediately by rearing up on its four hind legs and making what I can only describe as a short hissing or spitting sound. It raised its two front legs far above its head, and its pincers or fangs stiffened. I felt sure it was going to strike the fatal bite to my leg, but it didn't. It also didn't back off or run away in flight. Each of us just remained frozen in our respective attack positions for a few moments, as though we were a prehistoric display in a natural history museum. Each of us was prepared to strike, but we also appeared to be waiting for the other to make the first deadly move. In a sense, we were two deadly forces facing one another on a battlefield locked in a stand-off, as we contemplated our respective military strategies.

Contemplating—that was the word that had come to my mind again and again, and it only reinforced my gut impression that the spider I faced was fully sentient and intelligent. I could feel it thinking with every move and countermove it made. I decided to relieve the pressure between us to see how it would respond. I slowly lowered the knife and reclined back against the wall, assuming a less threatening stance. Likewise, the spider responded by lowering its legs and resuming its original contemplative stance. When I briefly raised the knife a second time to make it think I was taking advantage of its lowered guard, it reared up as before, but did not hiss.

I got the impression that the spider was not reacting to the knife as a weapon. It was unlikely that it had ever seen one before or had any knowledge of its lethal nature. Instead, the spider's response seemed to be measured by the degree of aggression I displayed by my actions. When I drew the knife swiftly and leaned toward it, it reacted in a more aggressively defensive way than it did when I merely raised the knife toward it. It made me believe that it recognized my second move as more of a bluff than the first, and did not consider it to be as serious a threat. It just matched me, move for move. We were testing each other's resolve and tolerance. In a sense, it seemed that our minds were trying to communicate.

I no longer felt any immediate threat from the spider. I casually relaxed and sheathed my knife. I then raised my empty hand with my fingers outstretched to show that I meant it no physical harm. The spider settled back into its casual stance. I readjusted my body slightly so that I could rest more leisurely on the entrance wall, all the while keeping my left hand on the wound it had given me. I ran my right hand down my chest and down my right leg to brush the dust off my clothes, then looked up at the spider plaintively and asked out loud, "Okay, now what do we do next?"

The spider didn't immediately react to my actions or words. I doubted it could hear me, and I knew it couldn't speak, but I wanted to make it feel that I was at ease with its presence. I calmly watched as it took a few hesitant steps toward me. When it was finally standing almost immediately adjacent to my outstretched right leg, it stopped. I made no reaction to its approach, which appeared to reassure it that I was no longer frightened by it. So far, so good.

Several seconds later, it slowly lifted its left front leg and set it down gently on my right leg. I felt it apply just enough pressure to rock my leg back and forth on the ground for just a moment, then it withdrew and resumed its casual stance. Was it asking me if I was okay? Was it testing me in some way? Was it prompting me to stand up? I got the distinct impression from the move that it had no intention to seriously hurt me when it stung my left ankle. Perhaps it was doing what it thought was prudent to wake me up and get my attention.

The fact that my mind was working to understand each of its carefully measured actions confirmed to me that we were actively trying to communicate with each other. This was *not* an animal whose mind and actions were governed solely by instinct. I recalled learning, when I was a child, that a number of other animals had demonstrated they were capable of conscious thought—among them were apes, dolphins and crows. There was no room for doubt in my mind any longer. The spider was a thinking being, and it was fully aware that I was, too. It was clearly sentient, and it wanted me to understand that.

The spider's next move intrigued me. I watched as it lifted its right front leg and lightly tapped the floor with it—not once, but four consecutive times. Several seconds later, it repeated the move, clearly tapping its foot four times on the ground—no more and no less. I gave it a puzzled look. Was it trying to tell me something or was it asking me something? What could the number four mean to it? For that matter, what could *any* number mean to a simple spider? But, then again, virtually all spiders obviously possessed some innate understanding of basic geometry and engineering principles in order to build webs that were so intricately and precisely designed to have maximum strength and durability. I wondered to myself, how bold a leap in intellect from that innate knowledge base would be necessary for it to gain a rudimentary understanding of numbers?

My first thought was that it was a reference to one of its pair of four green eyes. I could find no other immediately apparent meaning for the number four. By this point in time, my mind was becoming so focused on our communication attempts that I began to lose track of the burning pain in my ankle.

In an attempt to reply, I raised my right hand to my face and pointed at my two eyes. I then displayed two fingers, then clenched my fist and rapped lightly on the floor twice. Sensing no immediate reaction, I repeated my move and nodded my head to affirm my attempt at communication. The spider shifted back slightly, apparently contemplating our communication gap and how to close it. I watched as it again tapped its right front leg another four times on the cave floor. It then raised and extended it in the direction of the entrance. As before, it repeated the same moves a second time, as though confirming its mysterious message.

Four, entrance. What could that possibly mean? How can I understand the game of charades we appeared to be engaged in? Four, entrance—four, entrance, I repeated again and again in my mind. What on earth could the number four have to do with the cave entrance? Suddenly, I had a flash of insight. The spider must have seen us take shelter in the cave during the storm. There were five of us in our party. Four of them left through the entrance after the storm subsided. I was the only one who remained. Could it be asking me where they went, were they coming back, or was it wanting to know why I didn't leave with them?

In an attempt to convey my understanding of its move, I repeated it, only I held up four fingers before tapping the ground four times and pointing to the cave entrance. A moment later, I pointed to myself and then to the entrance. The spider took one step back and then forward in reply. I took that move as a sign of agreement and smiled. It appeared that the spider wanted me to leave, as the other four members of my party had done earlier. In its mind, I was an unwelcome intruder.

Could that have been why the spider bit me—just enough to hurt, but not enough to kill? Did it only want me to leave? It all made sense. The pain it caused would be an effective way to frighten off an intruder, and its offensive stance at any attempt I made to defend my position seemed to be a measured way to convey its determination to defend the cave—its home. Everything it had done seemed consistent with my interpretation. The spider was sending an explicitly coherent message.

There was only one problem to my compliance with the spider's request. The sting I had received from the spider was painful and had numbed my foot. At my age, I could not easily or safely climb down the rubble pile from the entrance by myself with only one good leg. To convey my problem, I raised my left pants leg, revealing the dark, red welt the spider's venom had caused. I pointed to it and winced to express the sense of pain. I then raised my left leg into the air, so it could see my foot dangling limply. The spider stood motionless for a few seconds, then shifted one step backward and forward, as it had done before.

Once again, I sensed that we had achieved an understanding. It seemed to comprehend that I had one good leg, but I couldn't simply comply with its request without support from my injured leg. I started thinking about what I could do next to resolve our dilemma and how I could convey it to the spider. It appeared as though the spider was also patiently contemplating our mutual problem.

A moment later, I heard a voice from outside the cave. It was Trevor calling to me that they had retrieved the horses, and they were ready to leave. The spider did not react to the call. When I gave no reply, Trevor called to me again. Once more, the spider didn't move. At that point, I realized that it could not hear. That told me that I could shout back without startling it.

"Trevor!" I called, trying to keep my voice as low as I could and still be heard at the base of the rubble pile. The spider remained motionless. "I've got a problem, here, and I'll need help getting down from the cave. Please come up to the entrance and bring Matthew and Junior with you. Let Jeffrey keep the horses until we can get back down."

Sensing that there was a serious problem, Trevor replied, "Hang tight. We'll be right there."

Within a minute, I could hear the sounds of Trevor, Matthew, and Junior scaling the rock ledge together. They were scrambling up so quickly that they dislodged a number of large, loose rocks with their feet, which went tumbling down the rubble pile. As the first few rocks tumbled down, I noticed that the spider flinched and began to slowly back away from me and the ledge.

Again, another moment of intuitive insight struck me. The spider couldn't *hear* the men or their voices, but it could *feel* the subtle vibrations caused by the rocks as they tumbled down the face of the pile. I instantly remembered why spiders always remained in their webs when they hunted. It was so they could feel the vibrations of the strands when an insect struggled to escape the sticky web. These giant spiders didn't build webs to help them hunt, but they could detect the most subtle vibrations in the ground or a tree branch to know when they were being approached.

As soon as the men reached the entrance, they saw the giant spider standing beside me. "SPIDER!" shouted Matthew, as he immediately recognized the creature that stood before him.

Almost by instinct, Junior quickly raised and leveled the rifle he had carried with him at the spider. The spider instantly shifted to face Junior, reared up in reaction to Junior's sudden move and hissed.

"*DON'T SHOOT!*" I shouted at the top of my lungs, as I raised my body and my right hand to block his aim. "It's not dangerous."

Junior lowered his gun and relaxed slightly. Each of the men had stunned looks on their faces as they absorbed the scene. When Junior lowered his rifle, the spider again settled down.

"It's okay. It bit me in the ankle, but it doesn't want to kill me. I think it just wants to protect its home—just as you tried to do, Junior, when we appeared at your cabin. It wants me to leave, but I don't think I can climb down the rock face on my own. I'm going to need some help. Please, come up to me slowly, and don't make any sudden or threatening moves. Since it first bit me to get my attention, it hasn't taken any aggressive action against me. I'm convinced that it will not attack, if we don't do anything that would make it feel threatened. Trust me, don't do anything that might provoke it and everything will be fine."

I decided not to tell them how intelligent I felt the spider was. It was still hard for me to comprehend, and I didn't know if I could convince them to accept it. I just used my hands to keep their movements slow and calm as they sat down beside me. The spider continued to patiently watch and stand its ground.

"Just set the rifle down, Junior. We don't need it. I know it won't attack or hurt us. It wants us to go, so it won't do anything to prevent that."

Junior laid the rifle down softly and began to look at the wound on my ankle. "I gotta get the poison out," he said. "Give me yer knife."

I slowly withdrew my hunting knife with my right hand and handed it casually to Junior. The spider watched motionlessly. Trevor and Matthew were stunned by its apparent indifference to our actions.

Working as quickly as he could, Junior ran the knife across the puncture wounds on the welt and sucked out the blood and venom, spitting it out through the cave entrance. He then ripped a sleeve off his shirt and tore a long strip down the length of it. He used it to wrap my ankle as tightly as he could tie it. "That oughtta hold for now, but I gotta replace it as soon as we get home. How bad is it?" he asked.

"It burns like a hot coal, and my whole foot is numb. I don't think I can stand on it, much less climb down those loose rocks."

"That's okay, Grandpa," Matthew assured. "You can grab onto Trevor's and my shoulders. We'll get you down safely."

Trevor nodded, as he stared at the spider. "Look at the size of it! How did it get here?"

I began to say I didn't know, when the spider turned around and walked slowly into the cave. Instead of turning right when it reached the bend in the passage, we watched it turn left and disappear behind a large boulder that blocked views into that corner of the cave. We hadn't looked behind that boulder, thinking that the cave only extended along the main passage to the right. Apparently, there was a smaller passage to the left hidden in the shadow of the boulder that we had overlooked.

Within twenty or thirty seconds after it disappeared from view behind the boulder, the spider re-emerged and started walking back toward us, stopping about five feet from me. We watched in awe as a swarm of smaller spiders—none larger than the one we found at the cold cellar—crawled out from behind it. We couldn't count them all as they packed in behind the adult. There had to be more than fifty of them in all.

"Lord Almighty," Junior gasped. "They's a whole swarm of them! Those little ones could've snuck up behind us durin' the storm and killed us all."

"They certainly could have, Junior," I noted, "but they *chose* not to."

Junior looked towards me and nodded in quiet concurrence. He then closed his eyes, and lifted his head to the heavens in silent prayer. I knew he understood. He shared our respect for life.

"It would appear that we're looking at its offspring," I suggested. "Just think about it, men. These spiders are too big and heavy to nest in a web like other spiders do. They must have to nest in a cave, an abandoned building, or a big hollow tree to protect their young. That's part of the reason why you haven't seen them, Junior. They've probably been all around you for years.

They just hide in places you don't look or that are hard to see. They have every incentive to do so in order to survive. Fortunately, they appear to have no instinctive fear of or animosity toward us. Given what this spider unintentionally did to my leg, I'd certainly like to make sure we keep it that way. I strongly advise that we leave them alone and not give them any reason to believe we intend to threaten them. I believe that, if we do, they'll let us go peacefully. It doesn't appear they want to pick a fight."

When the adult spider was satisfied that it had demonstrated its concerns to us, I saw it tap its left rear leg twice on the cave floor. That signal sent the entire swarm of juvenile spiders scrambling back into the shadows behind the boulder. The adult continued to stand sentinel, as Junior stuffed the flashlights into the side pockets of his pants and collected up the guns. Trevor and Matthew helped lift me up, and I wrapped my arms around their shoulders. We then turned and started our slow, careful descent down the rock pile. Jeffrey was standing with our horses at the bottom of the pile with a look of great anticipation and concern written on his face. I knew he would be riding next to me all the way back to Junior's cabin.

I never did look back at the spider when we left the cave. I had managed to learn everything I had wanted to know about them—and a lot more! I truly hoped our efforts to communicate with it and our willingness to leave peacefully and respectfully had convinced the spider that we meant it no harm. I also hoped it would assure its offspring not to perceive us as a threat to them. With any luck, perhaps we can find a way to establish respectful communication with them at some point in the future. Those inspiring thoughts gave me hope that we can eventually establish a mutual understanding with them based on peaceful coexistence. I would need to discuss that privately with Jeffrey, as I feel he will understand and work towards that future goal on our behalf. All in all, it was a *very* valuable trip.

# 15. Returning Home

With some support from Junior, I was able to mount Hercules. It was getting late in the afternoon, and the sun was hanging low on the western ridgeline. The air was fresh and sweet with the scent of spring wildflowers, as we resumed our determined ride down the abandoned highway to Junior's cabin. As I suspected, Jeffrey rode tightly by my side, and I treated him to a detailed account of my encounter with the giant spider. He discussed it with me excitedly all the way to Harman. I said we could discuss it in greater detail when we get home.

When we arrived at Junior's cabin, dusk was beginning to fall. Matthew, Trevor, and Jeffrey tended to our steeds and bedded them down for the night, while Junior helped me hobble into the cabin. He took me to his bedroom and instructed me to lay down on his soft feather bed. It was the first time I had laid down on a comfortable mattress in the past three days, and the sensation was truly delightful.

Junior carefully unwrapped the simple cloth bandage from my ankle. I saw a concerned look on his face.

"I gotta tell ya, Dave, it looks mighty bad. I guess I wasn't able to get all the poison out. The bite area has turned black. I'll put some salve on it, but if it don't look better in the mornin,' we may have to cut off your foot. I don't think you should be ridin' for a good while."

"Nonsense!" I insisted. "If there's a chance I might not recover from this, I want to go home. I can't die way out here in the woods so far from my family. We've been together too long and been through too much for me to do that. Please, Junior, help me get home as soon as possible. I can feel it's bad, but I can stand the pain and, if I can keep my feet in the stirrups, I know I can make it home. I just know I can."

Junior combed his fingers through his beard as he contemplated the condition of my leg and my words. "Yer a mighty tough cookie, Dave. I'll sure give ya that." He then busied himself by washing my wound, applying a salve, and bandaging it as securely as he could for the long ride home.

Due to the late hour of our return, our supper was light—consisting mostly of some leftovers from the previous day, supplemented with some cured meat from Junior's smokehouse in the back yard. My appetite wasn't very strong, anyway. Our supper conversation was subdued, due to Junior's news that my leg would never heal properly. Matthew and Jeffrey insisted that we cut off the infected ankle and remain with Junior until it had healed.

"Just what good would that do me, boys?" I asked. "It's a tough ride back to the farm from here. If I lose my foot, how easy will it be for me to stay in the saddle over the rough terrain? Also, if I end up staying here too long, the trail we blazed through Roy Gap might fill in again. If we leave now, we can ride all the way up North Fork Mountain without having to walk the horses. What's more, there's no assurance that my leg would heal even if we did amputate my foot. I like Junior fine. He's a good friend. But I intend to die at home with my family, not way out here in the woods."

No one had any argument with my statement. However, I did notice a tear in the corner of Jeffrey's eye. Somehow, I would have to make it up to him. I'd have to make him understand what it means to die with dignity.

***** *****

I had another night of uneasy sleep. My wound was beginning to become infected, and I could feel it burn periodically during the night. I also began to suffer from night sweats and chills. I didn't know how much life I had left in me, but I knew it wasn't the spider's fault. It hadn't intended to cause me any harm. It was just doing what it felt was necessary for the survival of its family—which was the very motivation that inspired me to undertake the expedition in the first place. In my experience, it's not the consequences of our choices in life that define our character; it's the integrity we display in facing them.

Jeffrey must have heard me wake up early in the morning. I heard him knock gently on the door and come in before everyone else had awakened. He had with him one of Junior's flashlights, and he shined it on my bed to see how I was doing. The nearly full moon shining in through the window beside my bed provided enough light for us to see each other, so I quietly asked him to turn off the flashlight. He walked in and sat down in the chair that stood in front of the bedroom window.

"I'm worried about you Grandpa," he began with tear tracks under his eyes. "I don't want you to die. Why won't you let us help you?"

"It's not that I don't want you to help me, Jeffrey. You just need to accept there's not much we can do. You're still very young. You've still got your whole life ahead of you. As for me, well, I'm 75 years old. I lived most of my life long before you were born. You've never known me as anything other than an old man. Even if I don't die today, I will soon. I can't live as long as you will."

"I know that, Grandpa. But I need you to teach me things I don't know. Look at everything you taught me about the meteor and the giant spiders. I didn't know anything about them a few days ago."

"That's true, but your dad and papa also knew about the meteor. I just happened to be the one you approached when you were ready to learn about it. As for the spiders, we've been learning about them together. I didn't even know about them four days ago. That's why I wanted you to come with us on this trip. I wanted to share that experience with you and your dad.

"Over the past few days, I've learned that you have a very inquisitive mind and a genuine and respectful appreciation for the governing power of nature. I'm very proud of you for that, and I know your dad and papa are, too. Those are the basic skills you need in order to teach yourself all the things I can't and to make decisions on your own. They also happen to be the skills you need to teach *your* children all the things they will need to know.

"At some point soon in your life, you'll have to begin doing all that for yourself. Oh, your family will always be there to help you—just as it always has for me. But, the important thing to understand is that if you just depend on us to keep making decisions for you and teaching you what you need to know, you may never become the responsible, independent adult that your children will need you to be for *them*. I see in you all the skills you need to be the kind of man I hope I was for you. I can't hold you back from that personal achievement in life.

"I know it's very hard to lose someone you love. It's also hard for me to face losing you, especially when I realize how much of your life I'll miss. I've tried to do my best for you and everyone else, but I can't keep doing it forever. Perhaps the only thing that makes it easier for me to face my inevitable death is the hope that I can die with dignity. I want to be able to know that I was a useful and valuable person to my family—not a helpless burden.

"I can't stand the thought of dragging my life out so far beyond my usefulness that I become nothing more than a vegetable. When I was very young, I watched that happen to my own Grandpa when he died of cancer, and it didn't make the pain of his death any easier to bear. It only made him suffer through a lot of pain that he shouldn't have had to bear. He didn't want to be remembered that way. There's no self-respect in that.

"Self-respect is not something that other people can simply give you; it's something you have to earn for yourself by the way you conduct your life and the way you treat those who depend upon you. The best way we *earn* dignity and self-respect is by doing as much as we can for ourselves and others—by being an asset to our family and our community. That's why we value our self-reliance and work so hard for it. You'll understand all that better when you get older. I know and appreciate the fact that you care so much for me. That's a source of my own pride and self-esteem. I hope you can let me die with that dignity and the knowledge that you're ready to become your own man."

"I'll try, Grandpa. I've seen some of our animals die, but it's just hard for me to accept."

"Remember what I told you the other day about faith. That's when you have to rely on your faith to relieve your pain and fears. Remember, we will all die of something, sooner or later. Death can be scary, but no single person's life is any more important that anyone else's. I've made the most of mine, and now I want you to make the most of yours. That's the best thing you can do to honor me and the life I've lived. It's hard to understand everything I've tried to tell you, and I may not be the best teacher, but I'm confident it will all make sense to you someday. Give it some time."

With that said, I sent him back to bed. I got a few more hours of broken sleep before the return of daylight brightened the bedroom. Matthew brought me some sausage gravy and biscuits for breakfast, which tasted wonderful. However, I quietly knew my strength was waning.

"We're getting the horses ready to ride, Grandpa. We decided to cut the horn off the front of your saddle, in case you can't sit upright for the entire ride. As long as you tie the reins together and you can keep your feet in the stirrups, you can rest comfortably and ride by leaning forward and holding onto Hercules' neck. We can even bind your hands around his neck to help keep you on him, if it becomes necessary. The saddle horn would only make that riding position uncomfortable for you."

"I understand. That sounds like a good idea to me. I didn't sleep all that well last night, and I've been having sweats and chills. That's likely to get worse as we go along, and I don't want my condition to hold us up. I want to get home as soon as we can."

"All right then. That's what we'll do. As you said at supper last night, the ride will be easiest if we can get through Roy Gap while the trail that we blazed is still clear. Aside from the steep terrain going over Allegheny and North Fork Mountains, that's the most difficult part of the ride home. We should be able to make a lot better time on the return trip. If you and the horses are up to it and the good weather holds, we might be able to do it in one long day."

Within another half an hour, we were ready to leave. Matthew and Trevor helped me get up on the saddle. My left foot was completely useless, and my ankle was very sore, but I was able to keep myself upright in the saddle. The weather was perfect for the ride—comfortably warm with light winds and a clear sky. We bade farewell to my good friend, Junior, and he presented us with a final gift—a poke[4] loaded with flashlights.

Our horses were in high spirits, and maintained a steady, sprightly trot along the open highway. It seemed that even they could sense we were approaching the end of our long journey, and were anxious for some relief. We stopped periodically to nibble on some food and allow the horses to drink and eat, but we didn't dally. We had satisfied our curiosity over the past few days, and we were all eager to get home and tell the story.

We managed to reach the Seneca Rocks Discovery Center around noon, and stopped for a mid-day meal. I had conservatively overestimated our original travel time, so we had plenty of deer jerky left in our saddlebag to quickly satisfy our hunger. We decided we would forge on in the afternoon, rather than spend another night at Seneca Rocks.

As I had suspected, the trail we blazed through Roy Gap was passable on horseback, as long as we rode single-file. The horses struggled to climb North Fork Mountain, so we rested again when we reached the summit. The view into Smoke Hole was glorious, and we relished the sight of Cave Mountain in the distance. We could almost see home.

We pressed forward and managed to arrive home only an hour after the sun had dipped below the summit of Cave Mountain. Everyone was surprised and overjoyed to see us arrive so early, just shy of four full days after we had left. I never passed out along the journey, but I did hug Hercules' neck during

---

4 'Poke' is a common Appalachian Mountain term for a sack or bag.

the ride up North Fork Mountain.  I wasn't sure I could keep my left foot in the stirrup because the trail was so rocky and uneven in places, but I managed it.

It felt good to lay in my own bed that night.  The cabin was quiet, but my leg remained very sore.  Laura checked it while Matthew was helping me get ready for bed.  She said very little as she rebandaged it, but she didn't have to.  I could see the concern written on her face, and I could hear some of her conversation with Matthew as they headed back to the farmhouse.  I heard her say my foot and a good portion of my leg is turning black.  I don't know how much time I have left, but I know it's short.  Now that I think about it, I can't deny that there is a certain amount of poetic justice in my death.  Although the spider never intended to kill me, I *did* kill one of them out of fear and ignorance.  Perhaps my life is a small price to pay to atone for my sin.  If my death earns me the right to join you soon, Clara, I can be satisfied with that.  You don't know how much I look forward to seeing you again.

I awoke at one point late in the night and decided to update the journal I have been keeping.  We rode so long and hard during the day that I had no time to collect my thoughts and record them since we left Junior's cabin.  I need to make sure it is complete before I do pass on.  I talked with Matthew about it during our ride, so he would know exactly what I wanted him to do with it.  I'm fighting my fatigue and pain, and it's hard for me to think clearly, as I write these words.  I think I'll set it aside and go back to sleep.  Perhaps I can write some more tomorrow.  It feels so good to be home again.

# Epilogue

I don't know if you can hear my thoughts, Grandpa, as I write them in your journal. Dad told me you wanted me to have it after you passed away. I recognized it immediately. I cried when he handed it to me.

Dad found you in your cabin bedroom, after Papa told him he didn't see you when he went out in the morning to milk the goats. You had passed away peacefully in your sleep on April 17—the night we returned—and Dad found the journal resting next to the candle on your bedside table. A pencil marked the page where you made your last entry. I want you to know that we laid you to rest two days later in the family plot at Cherry Hill Cemetery in Upper Tract, as you wished. We are still struggling with our grief.

I should also tell you that we had a visit from Junior about a week after we returned. He managed to track us to our farm. I guess I should have expected that of an experienced hunter, but I was still impressed that he found us. He said he came to see how you were doing, but I think he already knew what had happened. I took him to visit your grave, so he could pay his last respects. He knelt before your grave and said some words for you. I couldn't hear what he said, but I guess I don't have to tell you what it was. I'll let that remain between you and him. He spent the night with us before somberly returning to his home. We will be sure to look in on him from time to time. He has become a good and cherished friend.

I think I now understand why you couldn't explain your journal to me. Dad said you decided to make a record of the story as you told it to me because you knew you wouldn't be around to tell it to the next generation. You didn't want to tell me that you had a sense you might die soon. I feel proud to have heard the story from you and to have been part of our long expedition. I will carry those memories with me always and cherish them, as I know you hoped I would.

I want you to know how proud I am to be your great grandson. I always looked up to you and tried to be like you. When I read the passages you wrote about me, my interests, and my observations, I could sense the pride you felt in my accomplishments. I admit I never thought of myself that way, but it was reassuring to realize that you felt so strongly about me. I guess we just don't take as much time to express those feelings as we should. I hope you will always know that I love you. I'm sorry I didn't say that to you earlier.

I hope you won't mind, but I decided to add this Epilogue to your journal in my own words. I just had to write them down, so I could come to peace with my loss. I will honor your request to make this journal part of our standard homeschooling curriculum for future generations. I feel strongly that they need to understand and learn the values you taught me about nature and its role in our lives. I was saddened to learn that so many people died because they couldn't accept our place in the natural world. For a society that believed it knew so much, its demise must have been a crushing reality to face. In the end, all they could do was fend for themselves because they had nothing left to give meaning or purpose to their lives. If that's part of what you meant about faith and dignity, I want you to know that I do understand it now. You can't have dignity if you live without humility and hope, and you can't have hope without faith. I never realized how damaging an inflated ego can be. If vanity can ultimately destroy the soul, then I think we need faith and humility to strengthen it.

You can rest assured that I will tell all our future generations to be humble, to respect and revere the power of nature, and to learn all the lessons it has to teach us. I will inspire them to appreciate our farm, our way of living, and our spirit of self-reliance. I will teach them to value our family and all the love and support it has to offer. I will encourage them to work hard and take personal responsibility for their lives and actions. I will remind them to look for the good in everything, and to understand that adversity and hardship are not good or bad—they are simply nature's way of teaching us our limitations and how we should live within it. All these things and more I promise to teach them in your memory. If I understood your advice to me, I'm sure you would approve.

Like you, I have no idea how life will change in the wake of the meteor. I think you and Uncle Bob were right about the spiders. Please know that I did read and understand your final instructions to me about working with them to establish a meaningful, cooperative relationship. In time, maybe we can discover a way to communicate with them. I want to assure you that we will respect them and their intelligence, just as we would expect others to respect ours. Who knows which of us will hold the dominant role in nature eons from now? Perhaps their appearance signals a shift in the hierarchy of life on Earth. I don't think I can know what plans our Creator, whatever He may be, has for us or the spiders. All I can know for certain is that we need to change and expand our thinking, if we want to share *their* future and earn *their* respect. I also realize that spiders are *not* the only blue-blood species on Earth.

I treasure the time I had to spend with you, Grandpa. I hope that future generations of our family will gain a reverence for that sentiment by reading the pages you wrote. I also hope my own children and grandchildren will feel the same about me. I hope I captured all the important points you wanted to teach us through this journal. I hope you will always watch over me and help me make the right decisions in my life, just as you always did when we were together.

Thank you for all you have done for us. I hope I will see you again in my dreams. I won't belabor this tribute to you, because I know you'd want us to carry on with our lives. What's passed must remain in the past. Our future is what lies before us. Please rest assured, you helped me feel ready to take responsibility for it. I just had to say goodbye to you in my own words.

Here endeth the lesson.

*Jeffrey Ault* – *April 27, 2099 (old calendar)*

Made in the USA
Monee, IL
21 June 2025

19738392R10089